A Note to Readers

While the Allerton and Hendricks families are fictional, many of the people you will meet in this story actually lived. John P. Foote worked hard to bring art and culture to Cincinnati, and Robert Scott Duncanson was a free black painter whose landscapes were considered among the best produced in America during the middle of the nineteenth century.

William Lloyd Garrison was a leader in the movement to end slavery. With other people in the antislavery movement, Mr. Garrison worked to create stores that only sold products made by free people.

This wasn't easy to do because all the cotton gins—machines that separated cotton from seeds, hulls, and other material—were operated by slaves. A group of people opposed to slavery donated enough money so that they could buy a cotton gin to be run by free blacks and whites. Finally stores could buy fabric that hadn't been touched by a slave in any stage of its production. While this didn't put slave-run gins out of business, it became one more way for people to fight slavery.

FIGHT
for
FREEDOM

Norma Jean Lutz

PUBLISHING, INC.
Uhrichsville, Ohio

To Lorrie, Jadell, and Judy. Godly encouragers all!

ISBN 1-57748-257-3

Published by Barbour Publishing, Inc.
            P.O. Box 719
            Uhrichsville, Ohio 44683
            http://www.barbourbooks.com

 Member of the
Evangelical Christian
Publishers Association

Printed in the United States of America.

Cover illustration by Matthew Archambault
Inside illustrations by Adam Wallenta

CHAPTER 1

The Boy Named Damon

Two long lines of students stood waiting outside the large stone edifice of the Ohio Mechanic's Institute. Twelve-year-old Margaret Allerton—Meg to all her friends—stood on tiptoe to see over the heads of the taller students in front of her.

"Why are we waiting?" she asked her best friend and cousin, Susannah Hendricks. "Can you see?"

Although Susannah was only eleven, she was half a head taller than Meg. But Susannah shook her head. "Can't see a thing."

A taller boy in front, named Ellis, turned around. "Someone said Mr. Gallagher is at the doorway talking to President

Foote." Mr. Gallagher was the new fifth-grade teacher at Liberty School, and Meg felt Susannah was fortunate to have him. He was interested in art—something Meg had never seen in an instructor before. Her sixth-grade teacher, Mrs. Gravitt, was a stern-faced widow who wore nothing but black. Meg found that to be depressing.

"I wish they'd hurry," Meg said with an air of impatience in her voice. She'd anxiously awaited this day when the fourth- through eighth-grade classes would tour the galleries of landscape art newly hung in the institute.

She'd heard so much about Mr. John P. Foote, president of the Society for Promotion of Useful Knowledge. At a recent school assembly, Mr. Gallagher had explained how President Foote had aroused community interest in fine arts and mechanical arts. Meg stood on tiptoe again to see if she could catch a glimpse of what was happening.

Ellis looked down at Meg. "No reason to be in a hurry, Shorty. Just a bunch of boring paintings hanging on the walls. A painting can't *do* anything!" He gave a grin. "On our next field trip, we'll view the exhibits of industrial and scientific inventions. Now *that* will be something to see."

Ellis sounded much like Meg's younger brother, Fred, who was fascinated with anything mechanical or scientific. Fred teased her mercilessly about her love of drawing. He told her it was a waste of time, but she knew he was only echoing what Mama had said.

While they waited, Meg admired the towering maples and oaks that surrounded the institute. They were splashed with tones of gold and crimson, and the sunlight streaming through made each leaf glow.

Meg had been told that the botanical gardens were

designed especially as a place for art students to come and paint. Stone benches were strategically positioned along the walks among the shade trees. For a moment Meg tried to imagine what it would be like to be one of those students sitting there sketching. Sitting there, with all the time in the world!

"Meg! No time for dreaming," Susannah said. "Let's go."

Meg turned to see the lines suddenly moving forward and hurried to catch up.

The students were led up the outside stone steps into the high-ceilinged marble entry. Tall cathedral windows allowed the brilliant sunshine to flood in. Meg noticed how the light fell in geometric patterns on the glossy floor, but there was no time to study it now. The large group made their way up the broad staircase that led to the second floor. A short hallway opened into a spacious gallery where landscapes of all sizes and descriptions were hung.

Meg had wanted to come to the institute and see the galleries ever since it opened the year before, but there never seemed to be time in their household for such frivolous things. This field trip had excited her from the first day it was announced, and now she was here.

Still she was frustrated. The pushing and shoving of so many students made it difficult to spend time studying any one painting, and her small size prevented her from pressing her way to the front.

After unsuccessfully trying to view a few paintings, Meg discovered that lagging behind allowed her a clear view. The soft pastoral scenes were probably her favorites. Ones that portrayed sunlight streaming through the trees of a thick forest also fascinated her.

Then Meg caught sight of an ocean storm scene. The gilt-framed canvas was gigantic, and as Meg gazed up at it, she felt she was right in the midst of the crashing, breaking waves, feeling the spray from the breakers as well as heavy drops from the wild thunderstorm. Blacks, blues, and purples filled the canvas with power and excitement. How Meg longed to know the techniques used in such a fine work of art. But how?

In her bedroom at home, hidden away in the trunk that held quilts, was a stack of her sketches. But she dared not let anyone see them. Fred delighted in making fun of her work, and when Fred teased, seven-year-old Julia tended to join in. Mama wasn't much help because she believed drawing was a frightful waste of time. The frustration of it all made Meg's heart ache.

"Meg," said a soft voice beside her. "Mr. Gallagher says we're to move right along and stay with our group."

"Susannah, I'm sorry." Meg glanced about, shocked to see most of the students had moved into the next gallery.

Susannah looked up at the powerful oceanscape. "You like that one?"

"More than like. I can't even express how I feel when I look at beautiful art such as this. If only. . ." She gave a little sigh. "But then, 'if only's' aren't much good, are they?"

Susannah shook her head. "Like a cat chasing her tail. Going nowhere."

Meg looked back up at the canvas. "I may never see the ocean, but this artist not only allowed me to see this terrifying storm, but to feel it as well. Why, looking at this," she said, her voice going soft and dreamy, "I can almost hear the pounding thunder."

"I agree, Meg," Susannah said, "but that doesn't alter the fact that we must catch up with the others."

"Of course." Meg took one last look at the powerful scene.

As she did, a stern voice sounded from behind them. "Come along, girls. You were told to stay with the group. Please stop dawdling." Mrs. Gravitt came strutting along behind them like a cranky mama goose gathering up her goslings.

Meg's face burned. She was sorry she'd caused Susannah to receive a reprimand. Following Susannah out of one gallery into the next, she wondered what was the use of coming to the gallery if a person were going to rush through it.

"I believe there will be time for your art one day," Susannah whispered softly.

"I'd like to believe that," Meg whispered back as they joined the group of students, "but I don't see how. Mama's favorite saying is *Arbeit macht das Leben süss.*"

"And that means?" Susannah asked.

"Very simple. 'Work makes life sweet.' Though Papa doesn't exactly say so, I know he agrees." Meg gave a little sigh. "I don't believe Mama and Papa know anything except work."

"For some people, art *is* their work," Susannah replied.

Meg smiled. "Not my mama."

Later, as they emerged from yet another gallery, they came to the rotunda area in the center of the institute where the open balconies from the second and third stories looked down on the first floor. In the rotunda, Meg could look through the tall windows and get a better view of the formal gardens laid out toward the back of the main building.

As she turned about, she spotted a tall, lean young man

below her on the next landing. He had dark curly hair and wide expressive eyes. One hand held the railing, and the other was tucked into the pocket of his informal morning coat. Mellow sunlight played on the glossy dark curls, making them shine.

Beneath the boy's high cheekbones, Meg could make out the barest hint of whiskers trying to make a showing. The straight nose gave him the appearance of nobility, yet without a hint of arrogance. How she would love to sketch such a wonderful profile!

Quickly she tried to study the features so that later she might remember every detail. She was sure he was not with their school group. The way he stood looking out over the gardens made it seem as though he owned the entire museum.

"Susannah," Meg said, touching her cousin's arm. "Who is that boy on the landing?"

Susannah glanced down and shrugged. "Why just another student, I suppose." She then turned around and saw Mrs. Gravitt's dark scowl. "Whoops, time to move on again, Meg. We're heading for the last gallery."

Taking one look back at the dark-haired boy, Meg moved along with the group. How could her mind hold the details of all these paintings and still remember the chiseled face that she so desperately wanted to recreate in her sketchbook?

"Meg? Meg, did you hear me?"

Meg suddenly realized that Susannah was talking to her. "Did you say something?"

Susannah smiled. "No wonder Fred accuses you of dreaming all the time. I'm afraid I see his point."

Meg nodded in agreement. "I know. Isn't it pathetic? Yet I can't seem to help it. Fred calls it 'owling about.' Though

I hate his teasing, he's partially right."

A chuckle escaped from Susannah's lips. "Your brother has his own ways of owling. Only his head is full of noisy machines and smelly chemicals."

"Oh, don't speak badly of him, Susannah. Fred has such a keen mind." Though Fred was only ten, he'd read many books about the telegraph and steam engines, and he actually knew how a railroad locomotive worked. Meg knew about the bottles of chemicals he kept hidden in his room. In a way, she was very proud of him.

"You have a good mind, too, I might add," her cousin said firmly.

Meg sighed. "I'm not so sure. My mind seems to play funny tricks on me all the time. But let's drop all that." She waved a gloved hand as though to brush away the uncomfortable subject. "What were you saying when I was off owling about?"

"I asked if you were coming by the store after school."

Meg thought a moment, trying to remember what Mama had said that morning. Perhaps she'd not been listening. Giving a shrug, she said, "I'll ask Fred."

She and Fred and Julia loved to spend time at Hendricks' Mercantile, the store owned by Susannah's parents. But often Mama wanted them to come straight home and help with chores.

"Oh look," Meg breathed as she stopped at yet another landscape. This one depicted a French countryside where hay was being cut in the summer sunshine. Men in peasant garb stood near the ox-drawn carts loaded with golden hay. What techniques did the artist use to make the painting burst with the colors of summer? She might never know.

Susannah leaned near her ear. "You could do that."

"Don't tease with me." Meg turned from the picture. Once again, they'd been left behind by the group. She didn't want to get Susannah in more trouble.

"Why do you say I'm teasing? I've seen enough of your sketches to know you possess a keen eye and a steady, talented hand."

"But I've no inkling about the oils or the watercolors. How the colors are mixed and shaded. How light and shadow are created so perfectly." Now she was walking ahead of Susannah, lifting her skirts as she went.

"But we prayed, remember?"

Meg remembered. The two of them had prayed that Mama and Papa would one day allow her to take art lessons. Truth be known, Meg had no faith that such a thing could ever happen. The one time she'd asked her parents, Mama had quickly but firmly said, "Nein. Drawing der pictures is but a waste of God's good time which He gave to us." Papa agreed with her.

"I believe God will answer our prayers," Susannah continued. "Why, even my mama believes you are a gifted artist. She's praying with us."

"There are so many other important things for God—" Meg stopped in midsentence. There was the dark-haired young man. He was standing with Dr. Foote, seemingly in deep conversation. The two were standing in the hallway, gazing out the windows right where she and Susannah were headed. Meg's breath caught in her throat. How could she look at him and yet *not* look at him, all at the same time?

Susannah continued to talk about how God cares about the sparrows that fall and how He numbers the hairs on our head, so He surely must care about the little things in our lives. As her voice droned on, Meg's heart was thudding in her ears.

The young man's back was to them, and again she was able to see his profile and study his features, trying to burn them into her memory. Slowly, in ladylike fashion, they strolled past, and as they did, Meg heard Dr. Foote address the young man as "Damon."

Damon. Meg rolled the name around on her tongue a few times. Damon. She'd never met anyone by that name. It was the perfect name for a beautiful young man.

"Meg, this way."

When Meg looked up, Susannah was turning down a hallway to her left. "Oh, of course. How silly of me." She tripped along to catch up.

"You probably didn't hear half of what I was saying, did you?"

"Maybe half," Meg said, giving her cousin a sheepish grin. But her thoughts were still back in the rotunda with a boy named Damon.

CHAPTER 2
Fred's Fight

As the class walked back to the schoolhouse from the institute, Meg could hear several of the boys behind them taunting two young German girls. Meg recognized the girls as neighbors of her Oma Schiller. The two sisters, Hulga and Ida, like many of the German immigrants, spoke with heavy accents.

"Donkey donkey donkey-shane. For bitter, bitter, bitter shame." Over and over the boys chanted the singsong words.

Meg knew they were making fun of the German words *danke schön*, which meant "thank you very much," and *bitte schön*, which meant "yes, please."

Meg's Oma, or grandmother, used the words often. Meg's

heart ached for the girls. How thankful she was that although Mama's accent was slight, Fred, their younger sister, Julia, and Meg herself had no trace of a German accent.

"I wish someone would shush them," Susannah said softly. Finally, Mr. Gallagher came along and did just that. But Meg knew his shushing made no difference. The cruel words and jeering would simply come at another time—when no teachers were around. It was difficult to understand why one should be teased for being different. After all, didn't God purposely make each person different?

The field trip had taken up most of the afternoon, and school dismissed only a short time after they'd returned. Out in the schoolyard, Meg and Susannah met up with Fred and Julia. Julia ran up to Meg with a happy grin on her face. "We had a spelling contest, and I won," she announced.

"I'm proud of you," Meg said. She could picture her little sister boldly standing in front of the other second graders. Meg couldn't help but envy Julia's bubbly personality. Turning to her brother, she asked, "Fred, were we allowed to stop by the mercantile this afternoon?"

"Mama always says you never listen," Fred replied. Her younger brother had shot up in size the past summer, and now, at age ten, stood practically eye to eye with her. "Julia, tell your big sister what Mama told us this morning."

Julia stood up a little straighter. "Mama said we could stop by only for a short time," she said, proud that she knew something her older sister did not. "Because Mama is making the sauerkraut today and needs our help. But she wanted us to bring home a ten-pound bag of salt."

As soon as Meg heard, she remembered.

"Oh good," Susannah said, hooking her arm in Meg's.

"A few minutes is much better than no visit at all."

Susannah's older brother, Stephen, a seventh grader who towered over all of them, soon joined the little group. They all trudged down the street toward the city's business district, where Hendricks' Mercantile was located, chattering as they went.

Even though Meg enjoyed the store, her favorite part was the fact that it was right next door to Bushnell's Stationers. Often the stationer's window displayed art supplies such as colored charcoals, palettes, and large sketchbooks. Mama had taught Meg that it was wrong to covet, but Meg couldn't resist looking in that window each time she passed by.

The group arrived at the front door of the mercantile on Vine Street, laughing and talking. Stephen and Frederick discussed whether the coming of the railroad would be any threat to the canals or the riverboats. Fred was positive that the railroad was the answer to everything. Stephen wasn't so sure. Julia told all the words she'd spelled correctly to win the contest. Meg allowed herself to be carried along by all the friendly talk.

She enjoyed being around Stephen and Susannah. Fred seemed to act differently when they were with the Hendrickses. One time Stephen heard Fred teasing Meg, and he insisted that Fred stop. Meg wondered if Stephen ever teased his sister. If so, it had never been in her hearing.

Meg breathed deeply of the wonderful aromas that greeted her in the store—an odd mixture ranging from leather and iron to fabrics and books. Lucy and John Hendricks were busy with customers when they arrived, but Julia didn't care. She ran right up to Uncle John and gave him her usual friendly greeting. Nothing deterred Julia.

Stephen went to the back to hang up his hat and coat and put on his apron. Susannah invited Meg to come and see the latest *Godey's Lady's Book*, a magazine with the newest fashion plates on every page.

Susannah was fortunate to be in a place where new products arrived almost every day. The mercantile didn't carry many frocks or hats. As her father said, the dressmakers and millinery shops had that market. Yet they did keep a few things in ladies' fashions, and Susannah got to help her mother put them out on display.

Meg loved the bolts of lovely, new printed fabrics. Her favorites were the flowered prints on the calicos and the intricate weave of the bright plaids. Together the girls would try to figure out which fabrics would make up best into the new fashions featured in *Godey's*.

Just then Aunt Lucy joined them. "Afternoon, girls. How was school?"

Susannah kissed her mother's cheek. "Today was our field trip to the institute. No one was particularly thrilled about it, except for Meg here."

Aunt Lucy smiled. "Of course," she said in a knowing tone. "What did you think of the galleries, Meg? I've heard it's the finest show this side of the Alleghenies."

"I wouldn't know much about that since I've never been on the other side of the Alleghenies, but it was very nice."

Susannah gave a little chuckle. "How she understates, Mama. She swooned over every picture. It was all I could do to keep her moving and keep us from being scolded by Mrs. Gravitt and the other teachers."

Meg's face grew warm, but she was pleased she didn't have to disguise her love of art from Susannah or her mother.

"I understand some of Robert Scott Duncanson's land-scapes are in the display."

Meg shrugged. "We moved so quickly, I hardly had time to see whose work belonged to whom."

"Who's this Mr. Duncanson?" Susannah wanted to know.

"You remember," her mama said. "I showed you the article about him in the *Daily Gazette*. He's the black artist who came here from New York recently. President Foote hailed him as having great promise. His parents were slaves at one time."

"I don't remember," Susannah confessed, "but I'm sure Meg does."

Meg nodded. She remembered. She couldn't remember that Mama wanted a bag of salt, but she certainly remembered Aunt Lucy showing her the article about the black artist coming to the city. What a strange thing her mind was.

As they were talking, two little girls entered the store. Meg recognized them as the two sisters who were being teased that afternoon. Aunt Lucy excused herself and went to assist them. In their heavy German accents, the girls went over their list of needs, and Aunt Lucy politely worked with them.

Fred came back to where Meg and Susannah were poring over the magazine. "I have the salt," he said. "I suppose we'd better go on home."

"I wish you didn't have to leave so soon," Susannah said to Meg. "It's always more fun in the store when you're here."

Just then two older boys appeared near the front door, making fun of the little German girls as they went outside. "Listen to the porkers talk," they said. The girls pushed past the bigger boys, trying to ignore the onslaught. "Porkers, porkers!" the boys yelled.

18

Many of the men in the German community worked at the slaughterhouses and meatpacking plants. Meg had never liked the awful-smelling packing plants and was embarrassed that her Opa was part owner of one. But it was no reason to tease the little girls.

Meg sensed Fred tensing up. "They better stop that," he muttered under his breath.

"It's not your business," Meg warned.

"That's the same as poking fun at my Oma and Opa and that *is* my business." He handed her the bag of salt. "Here," he said. "Take care of this. I'll be back shortly."

Meg put her hand on his arm. "Fred, don't do anything foolish." But he yanked away and stomped out the back door.

Julia came running up to Meg. "Did you hear those awful boys? They were making fun of the way the German girls talked. I don't like that." She looked toward the back door. "Where's Fred going?"

"I'm not sure," Meg said. "Let's pay for the salt so we'll be ready to leave when he comes back."

"What do you think Fred'll do?" Susannah asked as she placed the magazine back under the counter.

"I'm afraid to guess," Meg replied.

"I'm going to take a peek." Susannah stepped to the back door and looked out. "My gracious. He's down the alleyway throwing rocks at those noisy scalawags."

Julia clapped her hands with glee. "Hurrah for Fred!" she cheered in her loudest voice.

But Meg was upset. What a foolish thing for her brother to do! Those two boys were bigger than him, and if they decided to fight back, Fred wouldn't have a chance. She paid for the bag of salt, took Julia's hand, and waited outside the store for Fred to come.

In a few minutes, Fred came tearing up the street from the opposite direction. Evidently he'd run off and then circled around to lose the other boys, who, as Meg had feared, had decided to attack him. He was panting as though he'd run for miles, but he wasn't hurt.

"Frederick Allerton," Meg scolded. "For shame. What kind of conduct is that for a gentleman?"

"A gentleman defends his family," he said proudly.

"Good for you!" Julia said. "It's not nice for them to make fun of Oma's friends. That would hurt Oma's feelings."

Sometimes Meg wished there were no Germans in her family at all.

Fred pulled out his handkerchief and wiped his brow. "A mite warm for an October afternoon," he said in jest.

Meg handed him the bag of salt and started walking down the street in disgust, but in just a few strides, Fred had caught up with her.

"You should have seen their faces," he said, his face lit up with excitement. "I got in a couple nice hits before they started to chase me. But I lost 'em right quick, weaving in and out of buildings."

"What if they hide and wait for you and beat you up?" Meg asked.

Fred gave a shrug. "It'd still be worth it. I'm not afraid of the likes of those bullies."

"Perhaps I should tell Mama what you've done."

Fred turned to her and grinned. "Perhaps I should tell Mama that you couldn't even remember we were to bring home the bag of salt."

Meg said no more.

CHAPTER 3

Attacked by a Rooster

When they arrived home, Mama was out in the back garden, pulling up the dead bean vines. She wore her cotton sunbonnet and muslin dress with a long shawl over her shoulders. Unlike Meg, Mama wasn't much interested in bright colors. Though Mama was not tall, she was large-boned and sturdy as a rock wall.

Meg studied the end-of-season garden. There were still carrots and turnips in the ground where Mama had banked straw to protect them from the early cold. A few tomatoes, which had escaped the first frost, hung on the withering vines, and the pumpkins were nearly large enough to harvest. That meant next week they would be canning the pumpkins. Soon they would pack the tomatoes in hay in the attic.

While they did not live in the German section of town, their home looked very much like those around Oma's house. Mama chose to grow a vegetable garden and a small orchard and to keep a flock of chickens, just as many of the German immigrants did. While Meg enjoyed the fresh fruits and vegetables, she didn't like all the hard work involved in keeping the garden.

Likewise with the chickens. She was thankful for eggs, but she hated pushing the ill-tempered hens off their nests. And she was terrified of the big rooster. Few of her friends at school had to work in a garden or gather eggs and risk being pecked by an angry hen.

Julia unhooked the garden gate and ran up to Mama, giving her a quick kiss and talking excitedly about the spelling contest.

"Das ist gute, Julia. You are learning well. But there is no time to dally about. Cabbages wait for us in the kitchen."

"Did you purchase all the cabbages you wanted at the market this morning?" Fred asked.

"All and more," Mama answered, pulling up another tangle of vine. "Plenty of sauerkraut we will enjoy through winter, until cabbages are ready once again."

Mama grew a few cabbages in her garden, but they had long since been cooked and eaten. At the Pearl Street Market, she purchased from the farmers all she needed for the yearly kraut-making.

Mama straightened up and tucked strands of her sandy hair back beneath the bonnet. Though Meg had inherited her

Papa's light blond hair and clear blue eyes, she had Mama's plain facial features.

"Fred," Mama was saying, "the crocks you will bring up from the cellar. Margaret will scrub them after the chickens are fed."

Meg wondered why Julia couldn't feed the chickens. She was plenty old enough. Besides that, Julia wasn't afraid of the rooster.

"From your school things you change now." Mama waved her hand to shoo them, much as she would shoo any chickens that came too close to her back door.

As Meg followed Julia up the narrow staircase to their shared bedroom, she found herself wishing she could have a long, leisurely talk with Mama. She longed to tell Mama, perhaps over a cup of tea, about the deep stirrings in her soul caused by the paintings hanging in the galleries. She wished Mama's quiet brown eyes would light up in excitement about something—anything.

Julia continued to chatter about her friends at school and the games they'd played at recess that day, but Meg barely listened.

"I'll help you feed the chickens," Julia said as they made their way back downstairs after changing into their cotton work dresses.

"Thank you, Julia. I'd like that."

The bags of grain were in a small storage room at one end of the henhouse. Meg unfolded the top of the muslin bag and scooped out the grain into two pans.

"Here chick, chick, chick," Meg called as she sprinkled the chicken feed on the ground around the henhouse. Julia took her pan and did likewise. The larger hens pushed the younger pullets out of the way as they greedily pecked at the feed, clucking softly as they went.

"Where's Mr. Cock?" Julia asked, looking about. Mr. Cock was her pet name for the rooster. "You don't suppose he's gotten out again?"

"I certainly hope not." Although Papa had built a good pen and Mama had clipped the wings of the hens and the rooster, the birds still managed to get out at times. Meg looked between the henhouse and the back fence. Then she looked underneath the wide back porch. There was no sign of Mr. Cock. She heaved a sigh of impatience. The weariness that sometimes crept over her late in the afternoons was beginning to make its appearance. She tried her best to ignore it and push on with her work.

"I suppose I'd best look in Mr. Mosby's yard," she muttered.

"I see him, Meg," Julia announced. "I see Mr. Cock."

Meg turned to see Julia looking through a bunghole in the back fence. Meg made her way through the garden to Julia's side. Her sister stepped back to give Meg a peek. Sure enough, there was Mr. Cock strutting through Mr. Mosby's flowers.

"You'd best hurry and get him before Mama gets impatient waiting for us to come help with the kraut."

If Fred were there, he could easily climb over the fence and grab that old rooster. This should be Fred's job, Meg thought bitterly. But then, she'd never be able to carry heavy crocks up from the cellar.

"Will you go with me?" Meg asked.

"You're not afraid of old Mr. Cock, are you, Meg?" Julia looked up with innocent blue eyes, her wispy brown hair peeking from beneath her bonnet.

Meg turned to lead the way across the dooryard to the gate. "Of course not. I just thought you'd enjoy coming with me."

Julia shrugged. "I guess so."

Together they went out to the front walk, around the corner, up the side street, and around to Mr. Mosby's house. Meg mustered all her courage to knock at the door. Tall Mr. Mosby opened the door and looked down on Meg and Julia. Meg felt tiny as a little ant.

"Yes? What is it?" he said. "You've interrupted my suppertime."

"I, uh, we. . ."

"Old Mr. Cock's in your flower bed, Mr. Mosby," Julia blurted out. "We've come to ask permission to enter your backyard."

"That blasted rooster in my nasturtiums again? Tell your ma the next time he's in my yard, I'm gonna make chicken and dumplings out of him."

Julia nodded as though the man had told a joke. "We'll sure tell her, Mr. Mosby, sir. May we go in your yard now?"

"Go on and be quick about it," he growled. "And don't be letting me catch any of you kids climbing any of my fences."

His harsh words made Meg cringe. But Julia piped up and said, "Our papa built the back fence, Mr. Mosby. That's our fence." Then she added, "Thank you, sir. Come on, Meg. Mr. Cock is waiting."

Meg echoed her thanks to their neighbor as well, but the door slammed shut, cutting off her words.

Julia lifted the latch on the gate and boldly walked into the flower garden. Mr. and Mrs. Mosby had had three children who had died years before in the cholera epidemic. Now it seemed the couple hated all children.

Julia wasted no time in running toward the back fence where Mr. Cock was scratching and pecking among the golden nasturtiums and marigolds. "Run at him from the other side, Meg," she said, "and he'll fly over the fence."

Meg wasn't too sure. But she ran and whooped just as Julia had. But instead of flying back over the fence, the big rooster flew at Meg. She froze in fear as the bird sprang toward her. She knew the pain that the rooster's long spurs could inflict.

Suddenly, Julia ran up behind the unsuspecting rooster, and just as Fred would have done, she grabbed him by his legs. "I got him, Meg!" she cried in delight. "You catch his wings."

Shaking herself, Meg willed her feet to move. As Julia instructed, she grabbed the flapping wings, and together they heaved the big fellow back over the fence.

"We did it!" Julia exclaimed.

Meg's mouth was like cotton. She could barely speak. "Let's get home," she said.

"We'll tell Papa tonight at supper that Mr. Cock needs his wings clipped again."

"Yes," Meg said quietly. "We'll tell him."

Papa usually came home for supper but stayed only long enough to eat. Then he would return to his furniture factory located down near the public landing, where he spent long hours working to make his company one of the best in the area. Handcrafted Allerton highboys, desks, poster-beds, and china closets graced the rooms of many plantation mansions all across the South.

During supper that night, Meg heard the story about Julia

26

winning the spelling contest as it was repeated for Papa's ears. He smiled his gentle smile and praised her for her accomplishments. Meg stifled a yawn, feeling almost too weary to eat.

As Meg listened, Goldie the cat rubbed on her legs, then rose up on her hind legs with her front paws on Meg's lap. Meg stroked the warm, silky head, wishing she could pull the cat into her lap. Goldie, who was the color of Mr. Mosby's nasturtiums, was Meg's friend.

Fred complained about the boring trip to the institute to see "dull old paintings," as he called them. "On the next trip, we'll view the industrial exhibits. I've heard they have a scale-model, steam-driven locomotive in the display."

Fred had read much about Matthias Baldwin's locomotive called "Old Ironsides." He often talked about how Baldwin's inventions had made steam engines safer and more efficient. This particular evening, Fred explained to his papa how a stationary steam engine could power the lathes in the factory.

"If your lathes were turned by machine rather than by hand, why you could turn out bedposts and chair spindles and legs more quickly than ever. Think of how production would increase." Fred fairly spouted the words.

Papa smiled and shook his head. Taking up the blue china bowl of cooked pork and cabbage, he spooned out another large portion. "I know that steam engines can turn lathes, Frederick," he said, "but not in Ben Allerton's factory. Nothing can surpass the careful hand and sharp eye of a man."

"But Papa," Fred began.

"Besides that," Papa continued, "steam engines are dangerous. There was another boiler explosion on a steamboat downriver just yesterday. The idea of blowing my factory apart doesn't appeal to me."

27

"Hundreds of steamboats travel up and down the river—some carrying Allerton furniture," Fred reminded him, "but only a few have accidents. What if no one ran a steamboat just because of the danger? Then where would our furniture be?"

"I have no say about the safety of a steamboat," Papa declared. "I have much say about my factory."

Mama rose to fetch the *Rehrücken*, a loaf cake that was Papa's favorite dessert. As she did, she glanced at Meg's plate. "Finish your meal, Margaret," she said. "Work is yet to be done before bedtime."

Fred glanced over toward his sister. "Meg always gets to feeling puny when there's work to be done," he said.

His words cut Meg deeply, but in a way he was right. It did seem that she grew sick a lot lately. Perhaps something inside of her didn't like to work. Could a thing really be so? She sat up straighter and attempted to eat, but the pork seemed heavy. She forced down a few more bites. When no one was looking, she slipped a piece of meat to Goldie.

Papa finished his cake and rose to leave.

"You will be late?" Mama asked.

"Joe and I must finish the inlays on the carved headboard for the order going out tomorrow. I will be late."

Mama nodded. She never argued about the hours Papa worked.

After supper was cleared away, Mama set up the kraut cutting board over a large wooden bowl on the table. In the center of the board was a razor-sharp blade that rose a fraction above the board. On this they would shred the cabbages to make kraut.

But first the heads were washed in a tub of water, then quartered. Meg and Mama and Fred took turns running the sections of cabbage over the blade. The work made Meg's shoulder and back ache. The shredded cabbage was then packed into the crocks and covered with brine. The kitchen was filled with the sharp smells of cut cabbage and brine.

Julia helped some, but eventually she curled up in the corner and fell asleep with Goldie pressed up close by her side. How Meg envied her.

It was late before all the cabbage was shredded and the crocks filled. Mama lay large plates over the tops of the crocks to hold the cabbage down. While Fred and Mama pushed the crocks out onto the back porch, Meg woke Julia and helped her up to their bedroom. Setting the glowing coal oil lamp on the desk by the window, she then helped Julia change into her nightgown. Julia was asleep again almost before her head hit the pillow.

After changing into her own worn flannel gown, she knelt down at the trunk at the foot of their bed. Riffling through her sketches, she pulled out a clean sheet of paper. Curious, Goldie came and rubbed against her. While the weariness pulled at her, Meg fought it.

"I'm not sure I remember him, Goldie, but I'm going to give it a try," she whispered.

Quietly, she pulled out the chair and sat down at the desk. She thought a moment before dipping the quill into the ink. Closing her eyes, she recalled the scene at the institute. She saw the light pouring in the windows and saw the boy standing there with his hand slipped into the pocket of his morning coat. She saw the straight nose, the small mouth, the dark curls.

Goldie jumped up on the desk and curled up on the corner. Meg rubbed the cat's head and ears and listened to the gentle softness of her purring. "You won't tell my secret will you, Goldie?"

Bending her head over her work, she began the sketch. The sound of the quill scratching on the page was as comforting as the sounds of soft purring. How she would love to spend hours and hours drawing and painting. What joy it would be to use oils to make a storm scene explode on the canvas. But she wouldn't even know where to begin.

Slowly the face on the page came to life. When it was finished, Meg was somewhat surprised. "Look at this, Goldie. It truly looks like him. Like the boy named Damon."

She could hardly hold her eyes open another moment. Satisfied, she cleaned the quill and returned the sketch to the trunk. Lifting out the quilts, she placed the sketch on the bottom of the trunk with the other drawings. Then she crawled into bed and fell asleep wondering about the boy named Damon.

CHAPTER 4

In Trouble with Mrs. Gravitt

The next morning broke sunny and warm. Meg relished every warm day, because she dreaded winter. The cold of winter seeped into her bones and remained there until spring. In geography they studied about tropical islands way out in the ocean where the sun shone and flowers grew year round. Meg was sure she would love to live in such a place.

As she jumped out of bed and put on her work dress, the sun was transforming the gray eastern sky into a pearl pink. Mr. Cock was crowing his heart out in the backyard.

After washing up and braiding her hair, she shook Julia

31

awake. It was her job to make sure Julia was up and dressed. Then she hurried downstairs to begin the morning chores. She was expected to help with breakfast and to feed the chickens and gather eggs before leaving for school. Aromas of *Kochwurst* and potatoes sizzling in the iron skillet blended with the smell of hot, strong coffee. Papa was already at the table reading a copy of the *Daily Gazette*.

"Good morning, Papa, Mama," Meg said as she came into the large kitchen.

"Gute morgan," Mama replied.

Papa looked up from his plate. "Morning, Meg. You're certainly chipper this morning."

She nodded and grabbed for the apron on the hook by the back door. "I slept well." She always slept better after she'd had time to sketch and draw.

Hurrying outside, she breathed deeply of the brisk morning air as she passed the garden and opened the door of the henhouse. She stepped back quickly to allow the birds to come running out. Sharp smells of chicken manure met her sensitive nose.

As always, Meg fed the chickens first in hopes that all the hens would come out of the henhouse. But it seldom worked. At least two of the cranky old birds wouldn't move no matter what. Taking up the wicker egg basket from the storage room, she moved from nest to nest, gently lifting the eggs from the hay. Some were still warm. Papa had built the sturdy chicken coop and all the nesting boxes that were mounted on the walls in straight rows.

"So," she said to the two hens who remained stoically upon their nests, "you aren't going to move." They glared back at her with beady black eyes. Some hens allowed her to reach right under them and take the eggs, but not these two. She stretched out her hand slowly, and quick as a striking rattlesnake, the hen pecked at her. She jumped back. "Grumpy!" she said.

Perhaps a stick would help. Setting down her basket, she went out looking for a stick beneath the apple tree in the far corner of the yard. Using the stick, she poked and prodded and shoved, trying to get the two old hens to move, but they continued to squawk at her and refused to budge.

"What would Fred do?" she muttered aloud. Neither he nor Julia were afraid of the old hens. Maybe she could use the stick as a distraction. Deftly, she moved up to the nest and waved the stick at the hen's head rather than her backside. As the hen pecked at the stick and kept squawking, slowly Meg reached out to slip her hand beneath the hen's backside. She felt the warm eggs. There were two of them. Could she grab both at once?

But before she could get hold of the eggs, the old hen turned and gave Meg two sharp, painful pecks on the hand. She jumped back, dropping the stick and grabbing at her bleeding hand. As she did, her feet became entangled in the wicker basket. The basket overturned, and Meg went tumbling.

Now the other stubborn hen joined the first one as they sauntered slowly out of the henhouse. Meg wasn't feeling too chipper any longer. Her hand was bleeding, and broken eggs were everywhere.

Just then, Fred appeared at the henhouse door. Through a thinly veiled smirk, he said, "Mama sent me to see what's taking you so long. But I guess I don't need to ask now."

Meg wrapped the corner of her apron around her hand. It stung like fire. How she hated those contrary old hens.

One part of her wished Fred would come and help her up. The other part of her wanted him to go away and leave her in her misery.

"What's the stick for?" he asked, still leaning against the door frame.

Meg tried to wipe egg off her legs. "I was trying to push the hens out. When that didn't work, I tried to distract them with it. But that didn't work either."

She silently righted the basket and retrieved the eggs that had not broken.

"I've told you," Fred lectured, "all you have to do is reach up behind their necks and pull them out. I've done that, and they never peck me."

"I wish you'd been out here to help." Meg tried to keep the bitterness out of her voice.

"I've been splitting wood for Mama."

Meg nodded. "I know." Of course he had his own chores to do.

Fred propped the door open with a board so the hens could go in and out freely throughout the remainder of the day. Then he turned to go back in the house. Meg slowly followed.

Mama frowned when she saw Meg's messy skirt hem. "The laundry is not done till Monday. Pour a little water in the basin and see if you can rinse der egg out before it dries. How many break?"

"I didn't count," Meg replied as she poured the water and proceeded to rinse her hem. The cool water felt soothing to her pecked hand. Now the awful weariness and dizziness were back again.

Julia came close to peer at Meg's hand. "Ooo, she really gotcha, didn't she?"

"Julia," Mama said, "come to bring platters to the table."

"If you just grab those old hens by the back of the neck—" Julia started.

"I know, I know," Meg interrupted.

"They know you're scared of 'em," Julia went on.

"Julia," Mama said more sternly.

"Yes, ma'am."

Fred opened the stove and shoved in another stick of wood. "Meg says she was so tired last evening, but I saw a light coming from beneath her door late."

"Meg?" Mama looked at her sternly.

Meg tried to find words. "Just a few school things," she said lamely. She wanted to ask what Fred was doing up so late, but he would only say he was making a trip to the privy.

"Drawing is more like it," Fred countered. "I bet she was sitting up drawing silly pictures. And after making like she was so tired. No one can believe a word she says." Behind Mama's back, Fred made an ugly face. Meg turned away.

Papa folded the newspaper and returned thanks for the food. As he filled his plate, he said, "The newspaper is still full of talk about the annexation of Texas. The presidential candidates keep arguing whether it should be a slave state or free."

Fred joined Papa at the table. "Do you think Polk would make a good president, Papa?"

Papa shook his head. "I have no idea. Don't know much about him."

"He was governor of Tennessee," Fred spouted, obviously proud of his knowledge. "And that probably makes him pro-slavery."

"Since everyone's heard of Henry Clay and knows him,

I suspect he'll win," Papa said.

"Well, I don't think he should let Texas become a slave state," Fred stated. "That's not fair. That just makes the slave states that much stronger."

Mama carried a basket of hot bread to the table. "Should not the day start before politics start at our breakfast table?"

Papa chuckled. "I guess politics goes on twenty-four hours a day, Emma."

Meg agreed with Mama. She didn't care to hear frightening talk about how the states disagreed. She wondered how her younger brother could be so sure of his own opinions. There were times when Meg wasn't quite sure how she felt about anything. She wrung out her hem and stepped outside to empty the basin. It sounded as though the clucking hens were laughing at her.

Mama rubbed salve on Meg's hand, then wrapped it in a clean piece of white cloth, tying a little knot to hold it fast. "You will please use more carefulness from now on," Mama said.

Meg wanted to say that she had been careful. But she didn't want to give Fred and Julia another chance to tease her about her fear.

Papa gave each of his children and his wife a kiss before leaving for the factory, then Meg had to hurry and eat since so much time had been wasted. Julia was already in her school dress.

"Mama," Meg said, "there's not enough time for me to help clean the table."

"Julia can help," Mama said.

"But Mama," Julia whined, "that's Meg's work. And besides, I have on my school dress."

Mama handed her an apron. "Not to be whining. Do as you are told."

Good, thought Meg as she hurried upstairs. It was about time young Julia helped out more. The thought made her feel guilty. After all, Julia was only seven.

She glanced out her window a moment at the bright sky that had set ablaze the gold and crimson trees. She'd almost forgotten how happy she'd been when she first awoke. Could that have been only two hours ago?

Standing before the mirror, she tucked loose strands of her blond hair into the braid, then fastened the braid up in the back with hairpins. She took her bonnet from the hook, put it on, and neatly tied the bow. Grabbing her shawl and school-books, she hurried down the steps as Fred called out, "Hurry up slowpoke or you'll make us all late."

On the way to school, Fred continued to talk about the elections, and Julia chattered about her friend Nettie. Julia and Nettie wanted to be friends with Amy, but Amy didn't want to play with them. Meg wished her problems were as simple as Julia's. She walked quietly between her two siblings, wondering how she could listen to both.

As they neared the school, two of Fred's chums called out to him. Fred left his sisters to join his friends. Meg didn't mind. Julia was always easier to be around when Fred wasn't there.

Susannah was waiting for Meg at the schoolyard gate. "I thought you were going to be late," she said. "It's almost time for the bell to ring." Spying Meg's bandaged hand, she said, "My gracious! What happened?"

"Meg broke all the eggs," Julia piped up, as though she were telling the most wonderful news. "She had to scrub out the hem of her work dress."

Meg glanced around the schoolyard. "Julia, isn't that your friend Nettie over there by the swings?"

"That's her! Nettie!" Julia called. "Hello, Nettie." And she was gone.

"Those awful chickens again?" Susannah said in a sympathetic voice. "I'm glad my mama doesn't want to keep hens."

"You should be. They're frightening creatures." Meg told about her adventure the evening before, rounding up Mr. Cock. "And Julia, young as she is, isn't one bit afraid. It makes me feel so silly."

"You're not silly, Meg, you're just. . .Well, you're *you*."

Meg looked at her friend. "If that's so, it's certainly not easy being me."

"Why doesn't your papa hire a domestic? I don't know what we'd do without our Bella. Mama goes to the store early with Papa, and Bella fixes our breakfast and cleans up."

"You know the answer to that, Susannah. Mama would never allow another woman in her kitchen. She says if she can't do it, it doesn't need doing."

Susannah shrugged. "And my mama says if there're eggs for sale at the market, why bother with the messy creatures?"

"How can parents be so different?" Meg mused.

The clanging bell interrupted their conversation. "Let's bring our copybooks out at recess and pronounce spelling words," Susannah suggested. Meg gave a nod of agreement as the teacher shushed the children and had each class line up in a row before marching in.

While Meg considered herself a fair student, she certainly didn't excel as some of her classmates did. Often her headaches and dizziness kept her from paying attention. Other times, she simply stared into space, dreaming. Usually she dreamed about capturing beautiful things on paper with the stroke of her quill.

As she listened to Mrs. Gravitt drone on about conjugating verbs, Meg's pen scratched out swirls and curlicues at the edge of her copybook. Could curlicues like the one she'd drawn become an ocean wave like the painting she'd seen yesterday? She glanced up from her scribbles to look again at the teacher.

Mrs. Gravitt's graying hair was parted in the middle and pulled severely back into a twist, with not one small curl in sight. Meg often thought that the woman must have been pretty when she was younger. But now the dull eyes and grim mouth erased that beauty.

At the throat of her black silk dress, the teacher wore a brooch with a small daguerreotype of her deceased husband. Mrs. Gravitt must have loved her husband very much to wear his likeness all these years. On her shoulder was pinned a small gold pendant watch on a chain.

Using a long rod with a hook at one end, Mrs. Gravitt pulled down the map of the United States. For the past few weeks she had woven the subject of the upcoming presidential elections in with their geography lessons, often pointing to the large Texas Republic, which was colored brown on their map.

"The candidate for the Democrats, James Polk," she explained, "is pushing to annex Texas and bring it in as a new state." Her face clouded as she continued. "However, Mexico has made it clear that she will never let Texas go without a fight. That could mean war."

Mrs. Gravitt went on to explain the problems of the issue of slavery. Some wanted Texas to be a slave state, and others wanted it to be free. But Meg had stopped listening. She sketched Mrs. Gravitt's likeness in her copybook until the bell rang for recess. It was a very good likeness, even if she had to say so herself.

Grabbing her copybook and retrieving her cloak from the cloakroom, Meg hurried out the door to meet Susannah by the elm tree. The area beneath the elm was one of the few grassy places left in the yard. The girls enjoyed their privacy for only a short time before Fred and two of his friends came running by them, kicking up dirt and teasing.

"Fred Allerton," Susannah called out. "You'd better stop it or I'll tell your papa on you."

"Are you gonna tell my papa on me?" mocked Fred's friend Aaron. "Ooo, I'm so scared."

Following Fred's lead, he ran up to them, stopped suddenly, then ran again, making the soft dirt fly up in a cloud.

"Pretend they're not even here," Meg suggested, and she continued to pronounce words to Susannah.

This made Fred dart in even closer. On the next run, he grabbed Meg's copybook. Before she could protest, he wheeled about on a dead run and ran smack into Mrs. Gravitt.

The copybook fell to the ground with the pages fluttering open to the picture Meg had drawn of Mrs. Gravitt! Meg felt her heart leap into her throat.

CHAPTER 5
Meg's Punishment

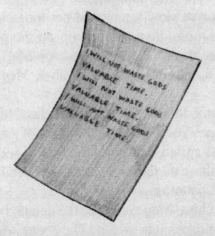

Everything seemed frozen in space for an eternal moment. Fred didn't move, Mrs. Gravitt stared at the picture, and Meg didn't dare breathe.

"Frederick, is that your copybook?" Mrs. Gravitt asked.

Fred shook his head and pointed at Meg. "It's my sister's."

"I see. Hand it here."

Fred reached down to pick up the copybook out of the dirt.

Taking it from him, Mrs. Gravitt said, "You run along and stop bothering other students in the schoolyard."

"Yes, ma'am," he answered. Fred was gone.

Mrs. Gravitt's tall, spare figure walked toward Meg and Susannah, her silks rustling. "Margaret," came the cool voice. "Please come inside with me."

Meg's throat felt so tight she could barely answer. She glanced at Susannah, whose face was filled with sympathy. "Yes, ma'am, Mrs. Gravitt." Slowly she followed her teacher into the schoolhouse with dozens of eyes watching her. Her face burned hot with humiliation.

Mrs. Gravitt slowly removed her long cloak and hung it in the cloakroom, then stepped up on the platform and sat down at her desk. She motioned for Meg to come stand before her. Looking up at her teacher, Meg felt small as a first grader.

"I presume this was done during class, Margaret. What a waste of time. You should be ashamed of such foolishness." Mrs. Gravitt riffled through the pages to see other sketches of Goldie the cat, fellow students, as well as myriads of designs and patterns.

Up this close, Meg could see the detailed etching on Mrs. Gravitt's gold pendant watch. The scene was of a graceful deer, with head erect, standing by the edge of a stream. Trees stood in the background. Looking at the etching was easier than looking at her teacher.

Mrs. Gravitt closed the copybook, placed it on the desk, and looked at Meg with steady gray eyes. Meg felt as though her teacher's eyes were boring right through her.

"I've noticed you do not pay attention well. Perhaps you haven't enough work to keep you busy. If that's the case, then you will be given extra work to be completed by the end of the week. As further punishment, you will remain after school this afternoon and write 'I will not waste God's valuable time' three hundred times."

Meg said nothing. She felt as though her trembling legs might crumble beneath her. In all her six years of school, she'd never been held after class nor scolded in this manner. And it was all Frederick's fault!

That afternoon as the other students left to go home, Meg remained in her seat. Several glanced at her with questioning looks. She tried to keep her eyes down. When the room was empty, Susannah appeared at the door of the classroom. Sizing up the situation, she boldly walked to Mrs. Gravitt's desk. "Excuse me, Mrs. Gravitt. Meg's brother and sister are looking for her. What shall I tell them?"

"Tell them to go on home. Margaret will be here for a time."

Meg could tell from the sparks in Susannah's eyes that her friend was angry. But what could they do? Susannah looked over at Meg, and Meg slowly shook her head. She pulled several sheets of paper from her desk to begin writing the sentences.

"Please leave now, Susannah. Margaret has work to do."

Three hundred times. It seemed an impossible task. As she bent over her work, she thought of the picture she'd drawn of Mrs. Gravitt. It had not been done in jest. It was not like the silly drawings she saw in the *Gazette,* which ridiculed the presidential candidates. But of course, she shouldn't have been drawing during class time. Why did her mind think in pictures? Why couldn't she listen in class like the other students?

The wooden seat she'd been sitting in all day was already uncomfortable. As time dragged on, and as she filled the pages with one sentence after another, her back and neck began to ache. The ache spread to her shoulders. She twisted about to find a better position, but there was no way to stop the ache.

Fifty sentences fit on a page. Six pages would be needed. After an hour, she'd filled only three and a half pages. She thought surely Mrs. Gravitt would want to go home. But Meg's teacher sat in her wooden swivel chair, her back ramrod straight, reading a book. Meg could hear old Mr. Barnett sweeping out in the hall.

She dipped her quill again and again. Fifty more sentences were done; one hundred more to go. She placed the quill down and rubbed at her hand and wrist, picked it back up, and began again. Mrs. Gravitt said nothing. The last fifty seemed to go more slowly than all the rest. Meg felt she could not move her hand to write one more line. The penmanship looked like chicken scratchings.

At last, in a small soft voice, she said, "The sentences are completed, ma'am."

"Bring them to me."

Meg wasn't sure her legs would hold her. She scooted to the edge of the seat, and using her hands, she supported her weight as she slowly tested her legs. They felt weak and rubbery.

"Please don't dawdle, Margaret. The hour is late."

Picking up the pages, Meg willed her feet to carry her to the desk and placed the papers on the teacher's desk. Mrs. Gravitt did not even look at them. "Let this be a lesson to you, Margaret. You come to school to learn, not to waste time."

"Yes, ma'am."

Mrs. Gravitt handed her a paper with a list of extra assignments she was to complete by the end of the week.

Extra problems in arithmetic, extra sentences to diagram in language, and a report to write. Meg stared at the sheet. She had no idea how she would get it all done.

"You may go."

"Thank you, ma'am."

From the cloakroom, she fetched her cloak, bonnet, and lunch bucket. Outside, twilight had covered the city, and the evening chill had set in. Meg shivered as she wrapped her cloak about her. It was not her heavy cloak because Mama hadn't yet brought the winter things down from the attic.

She lifted the latch on the schoolyard gate and made her way down the sidewalk toward home. Just then, she saw a figure up ahead leaning against the pole of the gas lamp.

She squinted her eyes to see better. To her joy and surprise, it was Stephen! She felt her heart leap. He'd seen her as well and was coming toward her.

"Hey there, Meggie. It's about time you came along."

"Oh, Stephen." She felt breathless. "What are you doing here?"

"Mama sent me to walk you home."

"She sent you?" Meg could hardly believe it.

Stephen smiled and handed her an apple. "Mama said you'd probably be hungry."

Because of the aching, Meg hadn't even thought about hunger. But the apple looked wonderful. It made a crunching sound as she bit into it. She savored the tart juiciness. "You came all the way back from the store? You didn't need to do that." She felt embarrassed at bothering him.

"Susannah told us what happened," Stephen said as they walked along. "She was worried about you walking home so late. So Mama sent me."

Eating the apple infused Meg with a spurt of energy, but the pain continued to nag at her neck. Mama was going to be plenty upset about the situation. But if she knew the Hendrickses had been bothered, she'd be even more upset.

"You needn't walk me all the way home," Meg protested. "I'll be fine. Really."

Stephen ignored the remark. "That Fred can be pretty ornery, can't he?"

Meg took another bite of apple and pulled out her hankie to swipe at the juice on her chin. She didn't like to think about the angry feelings she had against her brother. She knew she should forgive him, but every time she forgave him, he did something worse. "He's ornery," she agreed, and left it at that.

"What did old Mrs. Gravitt give you to do?" Stephen asked.

"Write 'I will not waste God's valuable time' three hundred times."

Stephen gave a low whistle. "That's a lot of sentences."

"Plus extra assignments to be completed by Friday."

"Mrs. Gravitt is about as ornery as Frederick," Stephen quipped.

The remark surprised Meg. They were taught never to speak of their teachers with disrespect. Her mama would have washed Meg's mouth out with soap if she'd ever made such a comment.

"I shouldn't have been drawing in class," Meg said simply. She tossed the apple core into the street where the roaming pigs would have it for breakfast the next morning. "I should have been paying attention."

"Drawing pictures in class isn't any more wrong than

grabbing someone else's belongings."

Meg knew he was referring to Fred. She wished he wouldn't say such things. She didn't want to think badly of her brother. "Papa says our teachers are always right."

"Teachers are people, Meggie. Just people. No person is always right. Mrs. Gravitt has her opinion; you have yours."

They'd turned off Liberty Street. She could see her house in the middle of the block on Everett Street. "I'll be leaving you now," Stephen said. "You'll be fine."

Meg wasn't sure about being fine. But she did feel better with food in her stomach. "Good-bye, Stephen. Thank you so much. Please give the family my best and thank your mama for me."

Stephen tipped his cap and turned to go back down Everett to Denman Street, where the Hendrickses lived.

Meg knew Stephen could have gone all the way to the house with her, but he didn't want to make the situation awkward. His kindness had taken the sting from the awful day.

CHAPTER 6
A Good Idea

Mama never flared up in anger. Still, her children knew when she was sorely displeased. When Meg entered the kitchen through the back door, Mama looked at her with stern, unblinking eyes.

"You are late. A daughter of mine made to stay after school? It is a disgrace."

Meg said nothing. She could hear Fred and Julia snickering from the hallway.

"You were punished?" Mama asked.

"I had to stay after school and write sentences."

"That is all?"

Meg shook her head. She pulled a paper from her books

48

and handed it to Mama. "I have this to do as well." Goldie came into the kitchen and began her incessant rubbing against Meg's ankles.

Mama pursed her lips tightly together and shook her head. "All because of the drawing nonsense. Again it gets you in much trouble."

So Fred had already tattled. Meg wondered what Fred had said about the incident. Probably nothing about his teasing and tormenting her and Susannah at recess.

Handing back the paper, Mama said, "This is not good. The oldest should set good examples for the younger." Mama wiped her work-worn hands on a corner of her apron. "Change your dress and shut up the chickens. Help with supper, then to your room you will go to work on this punishment."

More snickers from the hallway.

"One more thing," Mama added. "Saturday you do not go to Oma's, but Frederick will go instead."

Meg nodded. "Yes, ma'am." She was sure Fred would like having an extra afternoon away from all the work.

"Go now to change."

As she left the kitchen, Meg heard her two siblings skitter off down the hallway, laughing and giggling as they went. She ignored them and trudged up the stairs.

Actually she didn't mind missing her turn to walk to Oma's house on Saturday. Sometimes her grandmother could be out of sorts. And the walk to the German section of town on the other side of the Miami Canal always reminded her of her connection to that community—something she'd just as soon forget.

Goldie bounded up the stairs ahead of Meg, around the corner, and into Meg and Julia's bedroom. Meg closed the door and scooped the cat up in her arms. "Oh, Goldie," she said, burying her face in the fluffy fur. "I don't understand what's happening, but it's so frightening. How can everything get so twisted around?"

She stood a moment, soaking in the peaceful purring. Somehow Goldie always made Meg feel better.

"You'll always be my friend," she whispered in Goldie's ear. She set the cat down on the bed, quickly changed, and hurried back downstairs.

The chickens had already been fed, but Meg had to round them up from the garden and into the henhouse, which was no easy chore.

Fred and Julia came creeping around the side of the house. As Meg shooed the chickens and guided them with a large stick, she wondered why Mama didn't have the other two doing their chores.

"Look at me, Julia," Fred said. "I'm owling about—dreaming, dawdling, and dallying. Shilly-shally, poke and piddle. Frittering away the moments."

Meg turned to see Fred staggering around in circles, his eyes buggy, staring into the heavens. His singsong voice repeated: "Dawdle-dally, shilly-shally, poke and piddle." He staggered about until he stumbled and went crashing into the dead tomato vines. "Whoa! Owling about is terribly dangerous. It gets a person in all sorts of trouble."

Julia laughed brightly at his antics. Fred knew he had a captive audience in his younger sister. She did everything she could to please him.

"Get up, Fred," she squealed. "Get up and owl about some more."

"What?" he said, cupping his hand to his ear. "Speak up.

Pokey piddlers can't hear too well."

This sent Julia into peals of laughter. "Pokey piddler, pokey piddler," she repeated through the giggles.

Meg felt the heat rising to her face as she herded the last hen into the fenced-in area. From there she shooed each one into the henhouse and barred the door.

She couldn't bring herself to scold Fred or to even fight back. How she wished he could see that his behavior was no different than the boys at the mercantile who had tormented poor Ida and Hulda. Not even glancing in their direction, Meg returned to the house, leaving her brother and sister to their merriment.

Mama was quiet as Meg worked with her, cutting up the vegetables for beef stew and putting the heavy kettle on to boil. Meg mixed the flour and eggs for the *Spätzle*, then dropped the noodles into the hot boiling broth. Before supper, Mama unwrapped the bandage of Meg's hand, applied new salve, and bandaged it in a fresh, clean strip of white muslin. The pecks were still very painful.

When Papa arrived home, it was Julia who delighted in telling the tale that sister Margaret had been made to stay after school. Julia had run to meet Papa at the front door. Clear into the kitchen, Meg could hear her little sister's high-pitched voice.

"Meg drew a funny picture of Mrs. Gravitt," she said, talking fast as she usually did. "Gracious mercy, did Mrs. Gravitt get mad. Made Meg stay after school and write sentences. Everyone else got to go home. Fred and me came without her. She walked home all by herself. And it was almost dark."

Meg's humiliation deepened as she heard how the story was growing. When Papa came into the kitchen, Meg

51

cringed to see the disappointment in his gentle eyes. She felt she'd let him down.

"What's this I hear?" he asked. Papa always smelled of wood and sawdust, and now he had bits of golden sawdust on his eyebrows and his beard.

"Is so," Mama said. "What Julia says is so."

Papa looked at her. "Meg?"

Meg nodded and went back to putting the plates about the table.

"We always knew her drawing would get her into trouble, isn't that right, Papa?" Fred had entered the kitchen at that precise moment to put in another word. Fred talked about Meg as though she were not standing right there in the kitchen. And indeed she wished she were anywhere but there.

Papa didn't answer but went to the wash basin to rinse his hands and face, ridding himself of the flecks of sawdust.

After emptying the basin and drying on the linen towel, Papa came to Mama's side. "What is being done about the matter?"

Mama took the big potholder mitts and carried the kettle to the table. As she did, she explained both the teacher's punishment for Meg and the ones Mama had added. Papa nodded and took his seat at the head of the table.

Supper was awkward and uncomfortable. Although beef stew and *Spätzle* were her favorites, Meg could barely eat. Across the table, Fred kept mouthing, "Shilly-shally, dilly-dally." Julia stifled her snickers.

Papa had more news about the Polk-Clay presidential campaigns, but Meg heard none of it. Fred joined in the conversation, which at least meant that for the moment, Meg didn't have to put up with his teasing.

Meg was surprised when after supper Papa told Fred to fetch his coat and cap. "You're coming back to the factory with me. There's some sweeping you can do."

It crossed Meg's mind that Papa might have noticed Fred tormenting her, but then she quickly dismissed that idea. Papa often had Fred accompany him. By the time Fred turned eleven, he would be spending more and more hours learning the craft of wood carving and furniture making.

While Fred ran upstairs to fetch his wrap, Papa walked over to where Meg was clearing away the plates from the table. "You like your school, do you not, Meg?" he asked.

His question surprised her. "Yes, Papa. I like school fine." For the most part that was true. She enjoyed learning, but sometimes her sick feelings kept her from doing her best.

"Your mama never had as much schooling as you now have," he went on.

"Yes, I know."

"So you should be thankful for the opportunities that our school system gives us."

"Yes, sir. I am."

"Then you need to stop wasting time scratching out drawings and keep your mind on your schoolwork."

Meg wanted desperately to obey Papa and to please him. "I'll try," she said softly.

Papa nodded. His soft beard tickled her cheek as he kissed her. Tears burned behind her eyelids. She squeezed her eyes shut to keep them from flowing. She loved her papa dearly.

Meg released an inner sigh of relief when the front door closed behind Fred's heels as he went off with Papa. It wasn't really a bad thing to be sent to her room after the dishes had been washed and put away. However, the list from Mrs.

Gravitt now seemed longer and more difficult than when she'd first looked at it.

Goldie was curled on one corner of Meg's desk. The coal oil lamp sat on the other corner. The aching in Meg's shoulders and neck had moved to her temples. Periodically she stopped working and pressed her knuckles into her temples to ease the throbbing.

By the time Julia came to bed, Meg had finished all of the arithmetic problems and most of the sentences that needed to be diagrammed. The next day she would stay in during recess to finish the rest of her sentences. She was determined to have all the extra work finished by the end of the week, just as Mrs. Gravitt had ordered.

The next morning, as Meg gathered the eggs, she realized that her bandage served as an excellent protection for her hand. After scattering the feed in the chicken pen, she thought about the situation. What if she wrapped cloth about her hand every time before shoving out the old stubborn hens? Better yet, perhaps she could stitch together a thick mitt much like the pot holders she used to carry the coffee pot. She wouldn't tell anyone. She could keep the mitt hidden behind the nest boxes.

It was a splendid idea. She stood at the door of the henhouse and marveled that she, Meg, had had such a clever thought all on her own.

"You're not going to best me ever again," Meg announced to the two hens who remained on their nests. With the aid of a stick and her bandaged hand, she had them out of their nests in no time, and the eggs were gathered with not one being broken.

Susannah was at the schoolyard gate to meet Meg when

she arrived that morning. After Fred and Julia ran off, Meg told her friend about her idea for a protective mitt for her hand.

"You're much more clever than you give yourself credit for," Susannah told her. "What if Mama and I sewed the mitt for you?"

Meg thought about that for a moment. Although Susannah didn't say so outright, she knew how strict Meg's mama was. Mama might view the project as a waste of time and valuable fabric scraps. Somehow it seemed very important that Meg do this on her own.

"I'll sew it myself," Meg said, "but if you and your mama could give me a few scraps, that would be a blessing."

That issue settled, Susannah wanted to know every detail of what had happened to Meg after she'd arrived home. Meg told about the punishment Mama gave and about Fred's awful teasing.

Susannah rolled her eyes. "Why don't you smack that Fred a good one?" she said.

Meg just looked at her friend. The thought had never occurred to her. "I wouldn't want to hurt him. He's just being a rowdy boy. He doesn't really know what he's doing."

"I don't understand how you can let him get away with all that nonsense."

It was easy for Susannah to talk, but Meg didn't see what she could do. She felt completely powerless against all the orneriness Fred could think up.

"What did your papa say about it all?" Susannah asked.

"He asked me to stop wasting time drawing."

The first-grade teacher came out on the steps to ring the handbell as Susannah replied, "Margaret Allerton, you'd just as easy stop breathing as to stop drawing. It's in your very nature!"

CHAPTER 7

An Evening with the Hendrickses

Meg was able to finish her extra assignments and her regular schoolwork by Friday, but the coal oil lamp burned late Thursday night for her to accomplish the task. For once, her body seemed to cooperate with her determination.

On Saturday, she and Mama gathered the pumpkins and cut them up and canned them in large blue-green glass jars. Large onions were brought in and the tops braided together and hung in the attic. The remaining old vines and plants were pulled up and laid in a heap at the edge of the fence row. Only a few carrots were left in the ground and covered with straw to keep until the hardest freeze.

Fred was at the factory throughout the morning. When he came home for lunch, Mama made him change into his nice trousers and jacket and his Sunday cap before he left for Oma's house. Meg knew that although Fred never liked dressing up, he loved visiting Oma. He was her only grandson, and because of that, he was Oma's pet.

In the afternoon, Meg and Mama moved the heavy furniture in the front parlor and scrubbed the wooden floor with brushes and buckets of warm soapy water. Although Papa and his workers at the factory created fancy hand-carved furniture with scrollwork and inlays, most of the furniture in the Allerton home was plain. Sturdy, but plain. That was Mama's request.

Papa had asked Mama once if she wanted a nice rug for the parlor, but she replied that her handmade rag rugs suited her fine. "The cloth scraps are used up, and the girls' fingers are kept busy," she told him.

Making rag rugs wasn't one of Meg's favorite pastimes, and she wished they could have a soft flowered rug like the Hendrickses did in their parlor.

Julia helped some with the cleaning, but mostly she played in the bubbles. Taking a wooden spool, she dipped one end in the soap suds and blew until she had a mass of bubbles, then giggled at the sight. Later, when the golden pine floor was dry and rubbed smooth, Mama put Julia to washing windows.

By late afternoon, Meg felt lightheaded and dizzy, but she said nothing. She wondered if Mama ever became tired. Did she tire and simply say nothing, or was she truly as hardy as she appeared? It was difficult to tell.

Once every part of the house was sparkling clean, Mama

led the way to the wide front porch and it, too, was scrubbed—
as were the steps. Mama didn't even wear her shawl outside,
and the wind had turned sharply colder.

Every muscle and bone in Meg's body ached. What was
the need of so much cleaning anyway? One would have
thought the president was coming rather than the Hendrickses,
whom they saw several times a week.

Papa and Uncle John had been friends for long years.
Since they were boys, Meg had heard them say. And the two
families often spent time at one another's homes, especially
on Saturday evenings.

Before the guests arrived, Papa and Fred banked a roar-
ing fire in the parlor fireplace. The leaping orange flames
turned the room into a cozy sanctuary. After enjoying supper
together, the two families relaxed about the room, sluggish
from enjoying all the good food Mama had prepared.

Uncle John complimented Mama on her good cooking,
which made Mama's cheeks turn crimson. Meg watched
Mama and tried to imagine her as a young girl being courted
by the quiet Ben Allerton. Had she blushed back then?

Mama sat in her straight-back chair, mending Fred's
woolen stockings so they would be ready for the coming cold
weather. Aunt Lucy sat near her. In her lap was a pretty pillowcase on which she was embroidering a colorful flower
pattern. Meg petted Goldie and watched Aunt Lucy's needle
slide in and out. Goldie had made her rounds, rubbing the legs
of everyone in the room, and had opted to curl up where
Susannah and Meg sat playing cat's cradle near the hearth.

Papa and John sat in the bigger upholstered chairs in front
of the fire, and Stephen had challenged Julia to a heated game
of checkers. Sounds of the clicking checkers came from where

they sat at the small mahogany table near the bay windows.

Fred sat on the floor between the two men, playing with a handful of small magnets. He never ceased to be fascinated by them and had several large ones in his bedroom.

Uncle John never came to visit empty handed. Usually he brought along the newest abolition pamphlets or copies of the *Liberator* newspaper. Meg loved his ways of joking and having fun with everyone. She'd heard Papa say many times that with Uncle John's "gift of gab," he should run for a political office.

Uncle John pulled a paper off the top of the stack of papers he'd brought with him and shook it out in a display of mock importance. "Now folks," he said, "just wait until you hear what's about to happen in our fair city. After all these years of hearing about and reading about William Lloyd Garrison, we may have a chance to meet the man."

Fred brightened at hearing the name of the famous abolitionist. "Mr. Garrison? Coming here? Why?"

"It has to do with the boycott of slave-made products," John said as he opened the paper, searching for an article. "Remember when I told you about the Free Labor Association in Philadelphia?"

"They're the ones who've contacted the small farmers in the South and offered to market their goods," Fred said. "The farmers who have no slaves."

"You get an A-plus, Fred," Uncle John said half in jest. "A star pupil in civic affairs. The association has agreed to purchase all the free-labor cotton that the South can produce. And now they've even bought a cotton gin and sent it to a group of Quakers in Mississippi. They plan to hire workers to run the gin."

From across the room, Stephen looked up from the checker game. "You mean they'll truly have a product from the South never touched by slaves?"

His father nodded. "That's the idea. Garrison's paper reports that the orders are mushrooming."

"I suppose some of those orders will come from England," Aunt Lucy said as she clipped threads with her tiny sewing scissors.

Meg knew it stood to reason that Britain would get in on the market since that nation was opposed to slavery. She turned to Susannah and attempted to take the complicated cat's cradle from Susannah's hands, but it fell apart. They both giggled. Goldie playfully grabbed at the dangling string.

"But you haven't told us about Mr. Garrison," Fred said.

"Hold your horses. I'm getting to it," Uncle John said. "Garrison believes there are hundreds of small farmers and businessmen all across the South who are hurting financially because of the massive amount of slave labor."

Goldie stretched out and gave a wide yawn, her pink tongue curling as she did so. Meg rubbed the soft furry tummy. Goldie held the stretched-out position, relishing the attention. Meg had never really thought about small farmers in the South who had to compete against large plantations with slave labor. That must be very difficult.

"Garrison plans to come to Cincinnati and open a store that sells nothing but free-labor goods." The newspaper rustled in Uncle John's hands. "It doesn't say whether he'll remain here to operate the store. Perhaps he has other workers for that."

Papa shook his head. "Sounds impossible to me. No one can stock a store without having a few things made by slave labor. It'll go broke in no time."

Fred looked up at his papa. "If anyone can do it, William Lloyd Garrison can," he quipped.

Meg marveled at the way her brother joined in on the adult conversation. Most boys his age would be off in a corner playing with tin soldiers. But not Fred. Not even Stephen spoke up as much as Fred.

From over by the windows, Stephen called, "King me!"

Julia let out a loud groan. "How'd you do that?" she asked, studying the checkerboard intently.

"You don't pay close enough attention," Stephen replied.

"Ben," Uncle John went on, "it's not so much a matter of a store like this turning a profit. Personally, I believe it'll be profitable. But even if it fell apart after a year, its very existence will bring public attention to the plight of these poor people in the South who are suffering because of slavery."

Mama spread the trousers across her lap and studied the mend, smoothing it with her fingers. Meg wondered what her mother was thinking. Mama seldom if ever discussed civic or political matters with Papa. Meg watched as she took another garment from the mending basket and, finding the hole, began a new patch.

Goldie pressed her heavy body against Meg's side, purring noisily. Susannah began the cat's cradle once again.

"Your store handles scores of items made by slave labor," Papa countered. "If you believe in this concept so much, why don't you sell only free-labor products?"

"Perhaps I shall someday. But I don't believe in running ahead of where God is leading me at the time. It's Garrison who has the conviction to launch such an undertaking. And I, for one, admire him greatly for taking such a bold step."

"Me, too," Fred added. "I admire him. Do you think I'll

get to meet him, Uncle John?"

"I don't see any reason why not," Uncle John replied, folding the paper neatly and putting it back on the stack.

"We may be having a tea for him when he arrives," Aunt Lucy said. "We'd certainly want all of you to be there."

"Gracious!" Fred exclaimed. "William Lloyd Garrison right in your house. Can we go, Papa? Huh, can we?"

Meg noticed the troubled expression on Papa's face. "I don't know about all this, John," Papa said, ignoring Fred's pleas. "It appears to me that you're all borrowing a passel of problems, trouble, and heartache. You'll rile up the likes of those folks who dumped Birney's printing press into the Ohio River back in the summer of '36. Are you ready for that kind of violence?"

Meg tended to agree with Papa. Who wanted to stir up trouble?

"Some things are worth standing up and taking a risk for," Uncle John answered.

"Fred," Mama said. "Go fetch the popcorn and the popper. The flames, they are good now for popping."

"But Mama, I want to hear this."

"I'll go," Julia piped up. "Come help me, Stephen."

Long-legged Stephen, who was nearly as tall as his father, stood up and lifted Julia and swung her around. Her giggles filled the room, seemingly contradicting the growing tension between Papa and Uncle John.

"What good is it," Papa continued, "to say you are against slavery, and do it with anger and violence?"

John gave a shrug. "I'm not angry."

"I've read the Garrison materials enough to know *he* is angry. Stay around the likes of Garrison and his people, and soon it will rub off on you."

"Do you not believe in righteous anger?" Aunt Lucy put in, folding the finished pillowcase. "Jesus was angry when He drove the money changers from the temple."

Papa gave a wry smile. "I would leave the act of good anger in the hands of our Savior. I'm not sure many of us are able to emulate it well."

Stephen helped Julia to extend the long-handled popper over the hot coals. Soon the little golden kernels began exploding and giving off a delicious aroma.

Mama rose and went to the kitchen, returning with a wooden bowl full of polished red and yellow apples. Meg was thankful for the diversion. How she wished adults wouldn't fill the evening with such serious talk. She felt it was like a "sleeping sawyer."

On the river, the boatmen greatly feared a submerged bobbing tree trunk, which they called "sleeping sawyers." It could rip a hole in even the largest steamboats. Though the discussion between Papa and Uncle John seemed friendly enough on the surface, Meg felt as though a sleeping sawyer lay just beneath the surface, threatening to do them harm. How she hated violence and disagreements. Meg wanted everything and everyone to be at peace.

By the time the Hendrickses said good night, Julia was curled up asleep on a rug by the hearth. After telling Susannah that she'd see her at church the next morning, Meg helped her little sister get to bed.

When Julia was all tucked in and sleeping deeply, Meg placed a small quilt at the base of the bedroom door. Never again would Fred see her light on late.

With a clean sheet of paper, she began to sketch the scene

in the parlor. Susannah with the firelight playing in her pretty curls, Papa and Uncle John embroiled in deep conversation, Mama and Aunt Lucy with heads bent over their sewing. Fred looking up at Papa. Stephen and Julia at the checkerboard. Goldie, of course, stretched out before the fire. Herself, she omitted. The pen and ink sketch was fair. She wasn't sure about the shadowing. But it didn't matter much. She'd keep on drawing even if every part were done wrong.

Susannah was right. Meg would just as easily stop breathing as to stop her pen from drawing.

CHAPTER 8

The Accident

At church the following morning, most of the adult talk Meg heard concerned the upcoming elections. In a few short weeks, the nation would know whether Polk or Clay was to become the next president, and the subject was not far from the minds of most folks.

Because Cincinnati was situated just across the river from Kentucky, many of the citizens had strong sympathies with the South. Those who advocated the abolition of slavery were very much looked down upon. Meg was amazed that the Hendrickses were so outspoken about their feelings on the matter.

It was somewhat like being made fun of because you

were German and talked funny. As much as possible, Meg avoided putting herself in a position to be ridiculed. She received enough of that from Fred without asking for more. She couldn't understand people going out of their way to do or say things that would make others laugh at them.

The overcast day had turned quite chilly, but the stoves in the sanctuary were not lit so early in the season. Meg felt stiff and cold as the preacher preached on and on.

The evening before, Susannah had secretly delivered the scraps for Meg to use in making her egg-gathering mitt. Now Meg planned how she would cut it out and stitch it together when she was alone. She could see herself giving those big old hens a hefty shove with her protected hand. It almost made her laugh aloud to think of it. She hoped it wasn't vain to be so delighted with her own invention.

Sounds of rain slashing against the windows of the church competed with the preacher's voice as he drew his sermon to a close. Often when the weather was bad, the Hendrickses gave them a ride home in their carriage. Uncle John kept a team and a carriage, but Papa did not.

Meg was thankful for her sturdy bonnet and her parasol, which kept her from being drenched as she hurried to the waiting carriage. Uncle John took them home and then returned to church to pick up his family because there wasn't room for all of them at once. By the time they arrived home, Meg felt chilled to the bone. Uncle John joked that the first snow of the season was coming down as rain. It certainly felt cold enough for snow.

Meg enjoyed quiet Sunday afternoons. Her body, which could never keep up with Mama's strong, hard pace, received a well-deserved rest. For Julia and Fred, however, sitting still that long was terribly difficult. Mama and Papa had strict rules about the children being quiet throughout Sunday.

At dinner that day, Fred was once again talking to Papa about building and setting up a steam-driven lathe in the factory. One thing Meg could say for Fred—he was persistent.

Papa quietly, but politely, again told him no. No steam engines in his factory, he said. Meg could tell it made her brother most unhappy that Papa dismissed the idea so quickly.

"I'll be learning even more about steam engines this next week," Fred said between mouthfuls, "when our class goes back to the institute to view the industrial and mechanical exhibits. I plan to observe closely and learn every detail."

Meg had nearly forgotten about the second field trip. She wondered if she would see the boy named Damon again. Probably not. The building was very large, spreading over a good city block. And, of course, they wouldn't be in the art galleries this time. Still. . .

"Meg," Papa said.

"She's owling about again," Fred said with a smirk. "Her head is always in the clouds."

"Yes, Papa?" Meg answered. "Did you say something?"

"I asked you to please pass the *Schmierkas*."

Julia, too, began giggling.

"Yes, Papa." Meg handed him the bowl of a German cheese, much like cottage cheese, that he loved to slather on his bread. Papa hadn't scolded her for not hearing him the first time, so why did Fred have to pretend it was so terrible?

As they were finishing, a loud knock at the front door startled each of them.

"Who could that be on a rainy Sunday?" Papa rose from his chair and strode down the hallway to answer the knock.

From the voices, they could tell it was Uncle Bernhard, the husband of Mama's youngest sister.

Papa returned to the kitchen. "Fetch your cloak, Emma," he said to Mama. "Oma has taken a fall. We need to go."

Mama's face went pale as she hurried from the kitchen.

Fred was out of his chair in a flash. "Is Oma all right? I want to go. May I go along, too? Please?"

Papa shook his head. "Stay here and keep the wood boxes filled, son."

There was a flurry of activity for a few moments as Mama and Papa bundled up to go out into the cold.

"All work together to finish cleaning the kitchen," Mama instructed. "The rag rug I was braiding needs to be finished. Cold wind blows under our kitchen door, and the old rug is threadbare."

"Yes, ma'am," Meg answered. Braiding a rag rug wasn't how she'd planned to spend her quiet Sunday.

"Fred and Julia, help tear rag strips."

Fred groaned. "Mama, that's woman's work."

Papa gave a warning look. "You will do as you're told," he said. "Be sure the henhouse is shut up." Looking at Fred and Julia, he said, "You two mind Meg now. We'll try to be back before dark."

With that, Mama and Papa hurried down the front porch steps into Uncle Bernhard's waiting one-horse buggy. Suddenly the house was very quiet. Meg couldn't remember ever being left in the house without either Mama or Papa there.

In a tone as bright as she could muster, she said, "Let's get that kitchen cleaned up, shall we?"

"Go right ahead," Fred said with a scowl.

"Mama said 'all work together,' " Meg reminded him.

"You can't make me," he retorted.

Julia's eyes widened at this stand of defiance from her beloved older brother. "Fred, Papa said for us to mind Meg."

"You want to take orders from a pokey old dreamer?" he asked Julia.

Meg sensed Julia's confusion. She knew she had no power over either one of them. Returning to the kitchen, she took down the big dishpan and set it on the butcher-block table. She lifted the heavy hot water kettle off the stove and filled the dishpan. With a paring knife, she shaved a few pieces off the bar of lye soap and began washing the dishes.

Julia came into the kitchen and began helping as well. Meg could hear Fred grumbling in the hallway, but she couldn't make out what he was saying.

Once the kitchen was clean, Meg removed her apron, hung it on the hook, and thanked Julia for her help.

"You're welcome," Julia said softly. "Do I have to help rip up the rag strips?"

"You heard what Mama said just as well as I did. Let your conscience be your guide."

Meg went to the small front room next to the parlor, where Mama's work on the rag rug lay waiting. The parlor was kept closed off, except for when they had company. Meg went to the wood box, took several smaller logs, and put them on the fire. Just then, Meg heard a pitiful cry from Goldie. Running out to the hallway, she saw Fred pulling the cat's tail.

"Fred!" she cried. "Don't torment poor Goldie."

"I wasn't hurting your old cat. I was just petting her and she pulled away."

Goldie came running toward Meg, and Meg scooped her

up in her arms, cradling her and comforting her. How could her brother be so spiteful?

"I'm shut up in a house with two girls and a girl cat," Fred muttered. "What did I ever do to receive such punishment?"

Returning to the front room, Meg began work on the rag rug. She felt as angry as Fred did. If Sunday was a day of rest, why did she have to finish the rug? Julia sat on the floor beside her ripping the rags into long strips. Meg then stitched them end to end and braided them. The braids were then added to the rug that Mama had nearly finished.

By midafternoon, Meg's neck and shoulders ached terribly. Periodically she stopped work and stretched her arms and drew up her shoulders tightly, then released them again. The work was fairly swimming in front of her eyes.

"There are enough strips done now," Julia stated. "It'll take you awhile to catch up. I'm going to go play."

"You can help sew the strips together," Meg suggested.

"Mama didn't say I had to sew," Julia protested. "Only tear strips."

She was right. That's what Mama did say. Meg knew it was useless to argue. How Meg wished she weren't the oldest.

She rose to put another log on the fire. Soon it would be time for Fred to fill the wood box. Lifting the heavy rug, she spread it across her lap and continued the work. Another hour, perhaps, and the rug would be all finished.

The room was quiet except for the bits of wood falling and settling as the logs settled down into the soft ashes. Meg squeezed her eyes shut to stop them from stinging. It felt so good to let her eyes rest.

Suddenly, Fred and Julia leaped up behind her, growling, squealing, and making a horrid commotion. Meg nearly flew out of her chair, which sent them into fits of giggles.

"How can you make a rug with your eyes closed and your chin lolling on your chest?" Fred asked.

Julia could hardly talk for laughing so hard. "You really jumped, Meg. We scared you bad, didn't we?"

Would her pounding heart ever be quiet again? How long had she dozed? A glance out the window told her it would soon be dark. She felt ashamed that she'd not been able to stay awake.

"The wood boxes will need to be filled now," she said to Fred. "And while you're at the woodpile, please shut up the henhouse."

"I'll get the wood," Fred announced, "but the henhouse is not my concern. The chickens are woman's work."

Meg shook her head, trying to clear her mind. She was still shaken from the bad scare they gave her. "You will be at the woodpile, close to the henhouse. You'll already be out-side and bundled up. It will take only a moment longer to be sure the door is secure."

Fred acted like he didn't hear. "I'm getting my heavy coat, and I'll bring in the wood just like I was told to do."

What was the use? She might as well argue with a fence post as argue with her stubborn brother. In the distance, she heard the back door slam.

"Help me spread this out," she said to Julia. "I want to see where I'm at."

Julia took the other end of the rug, and they spread it out on the wooden floor. Meg would perhaps go around twice more, then finish it off, hopefully before Mama and Papa returned. If only she could keep going. Her whole body felt blanketed in tiredness.

71

"Julia, while I go out to close up the henhouse, please put on the tea kettle and lay out the cheese and bread for our supper."

Julia nodded her agreement.

Pulling on her clogs to protect her feet from the mud, Meg made her way carefully across the garden. The rain had turned to sleet, and the wind pulled and tugged at her cloak. Her breath formed little white puffs in front of her face.

The chickens were smart enough to stay inside, but the door still had to be secured. Otherwise little varmints could easily get in and kill the egg-layers. Meg pushed the door shut, securing the board over the metal hooks.

Coming out of the chicken pen, she saw Fred going in the back door with his arms full of wood. At least he was doing that much. Pulling her cloak more tightly about her, she hurried back to get out of the wet and the cold. A cup of hot tea sounded mighty good.

But when she stepped across the back porch and reached out to turn the knob, the door wouldn't open. She felt her heart lurch. What was happening? She rattled the knob and pushed. Nothing. A key was always kept in the lock of the front and back doors, but seldom were they ever turned. Then she heard Fred's laughter.

"Can't come in," he sang out. "Not by the hair of my chinny chin chin."

Now she could hear Julia's laughter as well. She tried not to panic. What would she do? How long would it take him to decide the bad joke was over?

"Unlock the door, Fred. It's cold out here!" Meg called, rapping at the door with her cold knuckles. She'd not even thought to pull on her gloves. She hadn't planned to be outside that long. "Julia, unlock the door and let me in. Right now."

72

But Fred and Julia were having fits of giggles. Meg stepped to the window. Fred was holding a yowling Goldie over his head as he danced about the kitchen table, whooping.

Poor Goldie. Meg looked about her, wondering what to do. She had to keep her head. Waves of weakness swept over her—whether from the intense cold or from fear, she wasn't sure. Perhaps she could slip around to the front door and get in while Fred whooped and hollered in the kitchen.

Carefully she stepped down from the back porch and made her way around the side of the house, taking measured steps to keep her clogs firm in the mud, while keeping her skirts up.

To her dismay, when she arrived at the front door, the giggles could be heard distinctly at the front door as well. What would Mama and Papa say if they arrived and saw her like this? Shame overwhelmed Meg. Knowing what she would find, she reached for the knob anyway. Locked.

Suddenly it was all too much. Her body shut down, and merciful blackness closed in over her. The last thing she remembered was a sharp pain shooting through her head and Julia's scream.

CHAPTER 9

The Exhibition

Meg opened her eyes to see two sets of frightened eyes looking back at her. Blinking a couple times, she realized she was on the floor of the hallway. Together, Fred and Julia must have dragged her inside. Her cloak was spread out beneath her. A cool cloth was on the side of her head. Julia was holding it there. Pain began to register. Sharp pain shot through Meg's temple.

"Margaret," Julia said in a quavery voice. "I thought you were dead!"

"Aw, I told you she wasn't dead, silly." Fred's blustery

front covered the fear in his voice. "Just like all women, she faints to save herself. If you can't get what you want, just faint. Poof!" He snapped his fingers. "Takes care of everything. All except for the knock on the noggin."

Meg assumed she must have hit her head on the porch post as she fell. She reached up to touch the side of her head, and her fingers felt something warm. She was bleeding.

"It's all right," Julia told her. "We got the bleeding stopped. I'll help you finish the rug. Are you gonna tell Mama and Papa?"

"What's she gonna tell?" Fred demanded. "We were just having a little fun. We didn't do anything wrong."

Meg struggled to prop herself up on one elbow. She had to get up. She couldn't be lying on the floor when Mama and Papa returned. Sitting up, she saw the drops of blood on the floor, as well as stains on her cloak.

"Let's get this cleaned up," she told them.

Julia jumped up. "I'll get the scrub brush and some water."

"Clean it up yourself," Fred fairly spouted. "I didn't make the mess." And off he went.

After they'd gotten up the blood from the floor and rinsed it out of the cloak, Julia suggested they take their supper into the front room and finish the rug as they ate. And that's where they were when Mama and Papa arrived home well after eight that evening.

Oma had fallen and her ankle was broken, but it was much better. The swelling was down, Mama told them as she removed her sleet-speckled cloak. Then she looked at Meg. "Margaret Allerton. Your head, it is wounded."

"I was shutting up the henhouse," Meg said. "I guess it was slicker than I thought. I took a tumble."

Not often did Meg have Mama's sympathy, but now Mama moved to inspect the wound closer. "Come, my little fawn. Salve and a bandage will make it better." Mama put her arm about Meg's shoulder, patting her in comfort.

Meg felt wretched that she'd not told the whole truth. That plus the fact that her head was still hurting. Mama's arm about her was such a comfort that she couldn't stop the tears that began to flow.

"Does it hurt?" Mama asked gently.

"A little." Meg hated crying in front of the entire family. Why couldn't she be strong? "The rug is finished," she said through her tears.

"Three willing workers make the task easier. I'm proud of you all."

Julia, who had followed them into the kitchen, gave Meg a funny look but said nothing.

The next day when Meg told Susannah about the incident and how Fred had behaved, Susannah couldn't understand why Meg didn't tell on him.

Meg gave a shrug. "He has a way of twisting things around. I was afraid if I told, he would make it sound as though I'd done something wrong."

"He picks on you more because he knows you won't fight back. You know that, don't you?"

Meg nodded. "I suppose you're right. But I'm not sure I know how to fight back."

Susannah put her arm about Meg's shoulder. "You're just too sweet for your own good," she said with a laugh.

The first day of November, election day, was cool but sunny. The newspapers were full of speculation about the election outcome, but the final count would not be in for at least two weeks. Fred was still holding out for Clay to be the winner. When Papa went off to go to the polling place, Fred reminded him to be sure and vote for Clay.

A few days later, Meg and Fred's classes took a field trip back to the institute, this time to see the industrial exhibits. Fred, of course, was thrilled. As the students walked in pairs along the sidewalk up to the building, Susannah said to Meg, "At least now I won't worry about you hanging back looking at all these exhibits. That is, unless you find something worth drawing."

Looking at all the colorful leaves strewn about their feet, Meg replied, "Almost everything is worth drawing, Susannah. Even some of the things I see in copies of Fred's *Mechanic's Magazine*."

While neither of the girls was particularly interested in inventions and science, still there were fascinating exhibits. They learned how Samuel Morse's telegraph worked and how a steam engine was able to drive a big steamboat up the river. A scale model of a railroad locomotive attracted all the students.

Meg found herself looking down hallways and around corners for a glimpse of Damon. She didn't really expect to see him again. After all, she knew absolutely nothing about him. But as she was passing by one of the tall windows on the second floor, she chanced to look out and there he was! Her breath caught as he emerged from a small cottage on the grounds. She'd learned from her last visit that the cottage was the home of President Foote.

She watched as the boy walked with purposeful strides down the sidewalk through the garden. He walked as though he knew who he was and where he was going. How Meg admired people who knew their own mind. Hers seemed so muddled at times.

She felt a hand on her arm. "I thought I'd lost you. Mrs. Gravitt told me to come back and fetch you." It was Susannah. She looked over Meg's shoulder toward the garden. "Did something out there capture your attention?"

Meg gave a sheepish grin. "I did it again, didn't I?" Thankfully the boy had disappeared from view. "The gardens are so beautifully laid out." She hooked her arm into Susannah's. "We'd better catch up before I get you in trouble."

As they moved into a large room and caught up with the group, Mr. Gallagher was explaining the McCormick reaper that was displayed there. "This machine can easily cut twelve acres per day," he was saying. "The machine is already changing the way the farmer reaps his wheat crops. We are looking at a glimpse of the future, when machines will do the work faster and more efficiently than men."

Across the room, Meg could see Fred with his fourth-grade classmates. His eyes were shining as he hung on every word. Fred might be ornery, but he had an inquiring mind. Meg didn't doubt that one day Fred would be inventing things just like Cyrus McCormick. That is, if Papa would just give him a chance. If Fred were busy doing the things he truly loved to do, perhaps he wouldn't make so much mischief.

One display that was especially exciting was a cylinder that stored electricity called a Leyden jar. The teachers had groups of the students hold hands. The first person touched the top of the Leyden jar while the last person touched the side of the jar. Meg let out a squeal as she felt a tingly shock go through her. The amazing contraption, along with other demonstrations of electricity, had everyone talking and laughing. Mrs. Gravitt had a difficult time restoring order.

"I wish Papa could see this," Susannah was saying as they filed down the steps. "Why he'd probably purchase one just to get laughs at the store."

Susannah went on chattering about the Leyden jar, but Meg no longer heard. On the landing stood the dark-haired boy. He was off to the side, letting the long lines of students go past. His eyes. Meg needed to see the eyes. She was on the side where he stood. She chanced one look. The eyes were wide and expressive. Dark brown, almost black, framed in dark lashes above the high cheekbones.

She was five or six steps above the landing. She dared to take one more look. This time the dark eyes were looking square at her. He smiled, then nodded. Burning with embarrassment, Meg dropped her gaze and carefully managed her long skirts as she went down the steps. When she arrived on the landing, she brushed so close to him she could have reached out and touched his blue velvet coat. Softly he whispered, "Hello."

Meg quickened her step and hurried on down the stairs with Susannah close by her side. As they arrived in the massive front foyer, Susannah grabbed her arm. "Meg, wasn't that the boy you saw the last time we were here? Have you been introduced to him? He acted as though he knew you."

"Now who has a dreamy imagination?" Meg teased her friend. "He was looking at everyone and smiling."

Susannah looked back over her shoulder. "What a handsome young man. I wonder who he is?"

Meg didn't bother to remind Susannah that she'd asked the same thing only a couple weeks earlier. At least now

Meg knew he was somehow associated with the institute.

"Girls, girls," Mrs. Gravitt said as she hovered behind them. "There'll be no more talking. Another warning will give you both a demerit."

After Mrs. Gravitt shuffled on past, Susannah mouthed, "We'll talk later."

But Meg knew there was nothing to talk about. She now had the face firmly in her mind and could easily improve on the first sketch she'd made. Whether she could imitate the light, life, and humor she saw in his eyes remained to be seen.

Since Mama needed several items from the mercantile, the three Allertons walked with the two Hendrickses from Liberty Street down to Vine after school. Fred could talk of nothing but the exhibits he'd seen. Meg had never seen him so excited. He was as full of energy as the Leyden jar.

Unfortunately, Julia overheard Susannah remarking about the boy on the stairway, and she demanded to know what boy Susannah was talking about. Meg gave Susannah a worried look. She certainly didn't want Julia or Fred to have another reason to torment her.

"Nothing," Susannah replied quickly. "Nothing at all. I don't know what you thought you heard, but I said nothing about any boy."

"Has Meg got a feller?" Fred asked. "Tell us, Susannah. Does she?" Fred slapped his forehead in mock distress. "That's all we need to make Meg owl about more—for her to be lovesick."

"You heard nothing of the kind, Fred," Susannah said. "Now hush your talking about your sister."

Stephen echoed his sister's words. "Let her be, Fred. She's

not done anything to deserve your teasing."

"Aw," Fred retorted, "everybody babies poor little Meg. She gets away with everything."

Meg sensed that Susannah was ready to say something about the bad bump on Meg's head, but Meg gave her a warning glance and shook her head. While she appreciated Stephen and Susannah standing up for her, it would only make things worse later.

As they passed Bushnell's stationers, Meg noticed a long rectangular box of colored charcoals in the window. On a small desk easel by the box was a still life of a vase of flowers obviously done in the charcoals. Meg hesitated for only a moment before hurrying by. How she would have loved to have lingered and studied the drawing more closely.

Later, as she and Susannah looked over the November issue of *Godey's*, Meg felt she needed to explain to Susannah about the young man at the institute. "I did look at him," she confessed. "But only to study his face to be able to sketch it. I never expected him to look back at me."

"Then I wasn't dreaming. He *was* returning your glance. And he *did* smile at you. Mm. And what a perfectly handsome smile it was, too."

"I didn't mean to be forward."

"Of course you didn't, Meg. I know that. But stop and think—he didn't know he was being an art study."

Susannah was right, Meg knew. She'd been much too forward and daring. It made her feel very ashamed.

"Make me a promise," Susannah said.

"What is that?"

"May I please see the portrait when you finish it?"

Meg hated to think about showing her work to anyone.

81

"It would hardly be a portrait, Susannah. Just a sketch."

"But you'll let me see, won't you? Please? Your own best friend?"

How could Meg refuse? Susannah had done so much for her. "All right. Yes, you'll see the finished sketch." How she would sneak it out of the house was another matter altogether.

CHAPTER 10
Meg's Secret

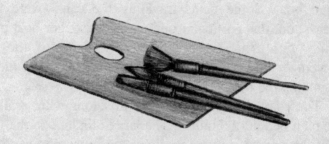

The next Saturday afternoon was Meg's turn to walk to Oma's for a visit. The German section of the city was bordered on two sides by the Miami Canal, so the community referred to the area as "Over the Rhine," after the famous river that flowed through Germany.

Oma often spoke of the beautiful Black Forest region east of the Rhine where she'd spent her days as a young girl. Meg was sure the Miami Canal looked nothing like the Rhine River in Germany.

Mama often commented that Over the Rhine was a place

more German than Germany itself. Immigrants clung to their language, customs, and love of food and music. While Meg enjoyed the friendly people, the growing prejudice in the city against all "foreigners" made her extremely uncomfortable.

Meg's basket was full of food for Oma, who hadn't been getting around as well ever since the fall that hurt her ankle. As she made her way down Everett Street toward the canal bridge, Meg heard the horns that the captains blew to let others know their boat was coming.

Meg stopped on the bridge to rest a moment and watched as the mules plodded steadily along the towpath, pulling the canal boat. Some boats traveling the canal were freight barges, but this particular one was a passenger boat painted white with trim green shutters. In spite of the chilly November day, several passengers were enjoying the view from atop the boat.

The young "hoggee," armed with a long whip, walked on the path behind the mules. The large blinders on the bridles kept the mules from being distracted by activities going on about them. The hoggee used his whip to tell the mules to stop and go or pull the boat over to the side.

As she watched the boats move lazily along the canal, Meg wondered what it would be like to travel on one. She could picture herself sitting on the top with other well-dressed ladies, watching the serene Ohio countryside glide by. Of course, she would be armed with a sketch pad in order to capture every changing scene.

But there was no time for daydreaming. Meg just hoped no one from school saw her crossing into Germantown. She didn't want to suffer the fate that Hulga and Ida faced each day.

Every shop in Germantown—each sporting German names—had window boxes where, in the spring and summer, flowers spilled over and brightened the scene. At the butcher shop, Mr. Ludwig, wearing a clean white apron, was sweeping his front steps. "Gute morgan, Fraulein," he called out to her, beaming his broad smile.

"Good morning, Mr. Ludwig," she answered politely.

Meg continued down narrow streets past the rows and rows of little shops. Men dressed in woolen jackets and blue worsted pantaloons called out to one another in German words and phrases. From somewhere inside a building came the lilting melodies of a mouth harp. It reminded Meg of the music she used to hear during long summer evenings at her grandparents.

When she was younger she often sat with her grandparents on the front porch, listening to music drifting down the street from the *biergartens.* Though Opa never drank beer, he loved being able to hear the hand-clapping, oom-pa-pa German music. He and Oma would teach Meg traditional dances. Meg loved the laughter and fun. But now Opa's gout didn't allow him to dance.

The homes in the neighborhood looked much like Meg's own home on Everett Street, with neat gardens and a few chickens and freshly scrubbed front porches. As she approached Oma's house, she saw that the front porch steps were spotless as ever. That meant that the neighbor women had given Oma a hand with the cleaning.

Tapping at the door, she heard her Oma's call to come inside. To her surprise, her short, stout Oma was up and about. Hobbling a bit, but doing well.

She greeted Meg with a kiss on her cheek. "And what

have we here?" she asked, looking at the basket. "Emma thinks her Mutter can no longer cook, does she? Ach." Oma gave a wave of her hand. "Up and about I am. You tell her." Oma led the way to the kitchen in the back of the house.

"I'll tell her, Oma," Meg said as she set the basket on the table and removed her cloak. Laying it over a chair, she began to put the things away that Mama had sent.

"Come, come," Oma said impatiently. "That work I can do when you are gone away. We'll pour coffee and visit. I want to hear all that is doing in your life. You did not come last week. It was your time to come, but Frederick come in your place. I like to see Frederick, but I miss your visit."

Meg seldom knew how to fit a word in edgewise when Oma was talking. Perhaps that was why Mama grew up to be so quiet. Sometimes Oma lapsed into long phrases of German that left Meg puzzled.

"You should speak der German, too," she would say in a testy tone. "You are German. Germans speak der German."

Now Oma poured coffee and diluted Meg's with thick cream and put in plenty of sugar. Slices of black bread were arranged on a tray and slathered with sweet butter. Meg helped pull chairs over by the fireplace in the small front room.

She never did explain why she hadn't come the previous Saturday, and evidently Oma forgot she'd even asked. Meg made polite conversation about subjects in school and the field trip to the institute. Her description of the tingling shock from the Leyden jar made Oma chuckle.

Then Oma asked, "You have a suitor at school?"

"Please, Oma. I'm not even thirteen. I'm much too young for a suitor."

"Ach! I was but thirteen when your Opa and I met and we married. If you lived in our community, I could introduce you to nice German boys. Good boys work at the packing plant. Your children could go to our German school, go to our German church."

Meg shivered at the thought.

"If only your papa hadn't taken our Emma away from us." Oma's voice became wistful, her pale blue eyes sad. Meg had heard Oma make that statement dozens of times. Always the same words, always the same sad tone of voice. It was as if Ben Allerton had kidnapped Emma Schiller and moved to another country. In Oma's mind it might just as well be.

"Is the fall butchering underway?" Meg asked, trying to change the subject.

"Underway, yes," Oma said in a brighter tone. "More hogs this year than ever before. Walford, he still thinks the packing plant cannot run without him. He will breathe his last breath standing next to a sausage stuffer, I suppose."

Oma had finished her coffee and bread and taken up her embroidery work. Sometimes Meg brought along her knitting or quilting pieces so the two of them could work together. But now that winter was coming on, daylight fled earlier, and the visits were much too short.

On this day, Meg excused herself even earlier than usual. She had a plan. Over her grandmother's protests, she put on her wrap and prepared to leave. Oma limped to her pantry to see what she could send back to her Emma's house.

Since both homes had the same of most everything, Meg wondered why her mother and grandmother even bothered. But it was always like this. Mama sent things to Oma's house, and Oma sent things back again. This time she chose two jars of her watermelon preserves and two loops of fresh *Leberwurst.*

In spite of Oma's protests, Meg made sure the items she had brought were put away before she left. After bidding Oma good-bye, Meg went down the same streets, past the same shops until she was two or three blocks east of the canal. From there, she turned and went south.

She smiled to herself. There was time before darkness fell for her to go to the institute and take a brief look around on her own. The galleries were free and open to the public. It was there for the citizens of the city. Why shouldn't she be able to look on her own? After all, she reasoned, Mama and Papa had never actually forbidden her to go and observe the art exhibits.

On the other hand, Meg knew that she was expected to go straight to Oma's house and straight home. And it was no secret that Mama thought art to be a wasteful folly. Still her feet kept walking south, across another canal bridge and farther away from her own house.

The vast institute complex was surrounded by a wrought iron fence. The gate was open. Excitement welled up inside her as she strode through the gate, hurried down the sidewalk, and entered the front door. The place seemed much different without a hundred or so students filing through. Could she remember where the galleries were? She especially wanted to see the landscapes. Just then, an elderly caretaker came out of an anteroom and asked what she was looking for.

"The landscape showing."

"Top of the stairs," he told her. "Down the hall, last gallery on the right."

"Thank you," Meg replied. It seemed so simple. So ordinary. Some people probably came to the institute every week or so to view each new exhibit and thought nothing of it.

Meg adjusted the heavy basket on her arm and went up the steps. Late afternoon sunshine slanted through the foyer windows and lent a mellow tone to each shiny marble step.

The sign outside the door specified the particular gallery she was looking for. This was the best way to look at art—alone and in the quiet. She went straight to the ocean scene and studied it at length. Taking her time, she strolled about the room, absorbing the beauty and detail of each painting. The oils seemed to be the most dramatic, but she loved the gentle pastels best.

Meg was determined not to make the mistake of overstaying her visit. Repeated glances out the window let her know where the sun was hanging in the western sky. When it was as late as she dare let it be, she reluctantly pulled herself away and hurried back down the hall. As she came to the stairs, the tall windows afforded a panoramic view of the gardens.

At the landing, she stopped still. A figure sat on a bench near a small bubbling fountain. Even though he was bundled in a hat and coat, Meg could tell it was Damon. Before him stood a large easel, turned so she could not see the work. Beside him on the bench were his palette and brushes. The boy was leaning back as though to study the work.

So now she knew. Damon was an artist. Or at least he was interested in art. Somehow the new knowledge made her feel guiltier than ever, as though all this rich goodness was too much for one person to contain in a single afternoon.

Down the steps she hurried and out through the heavy front

doors. She would have to walk quickly to make it home before Mama became worried. As she reached the gate, a voice called behind her. "Hey there. Hey! Stop! Wait a moment."

Meg turned. Damon had left his easel and was coming her way, calling out to her. There was quite a distance between them, so she hurried into a run, through the gate and down the street. Thankfully, he didn't pursue her.

What a fright! How embarrassing it would be to meet him. She couldn't imagine a more devastating event. She never wanted to *meet* him—she only wanted to sketch his likeness.

The last remnants of the sun were shooting salmon-colored rays across the sky as she arrived home. She went around to the kitchen door. Meg was exhausted, and her arm ached from the weight of the basket, yet deep inside she felt strangely exhilarated and happy.

Mama greeted her at the door, shaking her head and saying "tsk, tsk" at the sight of the *Leberwurst* and jars of preserves that Oma had sent. "I try to help your Oma, and what does she do? She tries to out-give me every time. How does a body help someone like that, I ask?"

Mama was in the midst of preparing supper, so Meg hurried to hang her wrap and put on her apron and lend a hand. Mama asked polite questions about her visit, and Meg answered them.

It seemed like a dream that she'd actually been to the gallery alone. Never in her life had she ever done anything so daring. Inside, her emotions were tumbling about. Surely she should feel sorry that she'd snuck off as she did, yet she wasn't sorry at all. It would take time before she could sort out her feelings. In the meantime, she had a new scene to sketch.

CHAPTER 11

The New Mitt

In the second week in November, the election ballots were finally all in and tallied. Church bells tolled as the news arrived that James K. Polk had been voted in as the eleventh president of the United States. Fred was not happy.

"Slave owners in the White House again," he groaned. "What a fine kettle of fish that will be. The South has all the power."

The morning following the announcement, he was still complaining loudly. Though Mama told him to shush since there was nothing he could do about it, he continued to mutter.

A skiff of snow had fallen, and Meg now wore woolen underthings beneath her heavier winter dresses. Pulling on her

91

heavy cloak, she went out to feed the chickens and gather what few eggs there might be.

Cold weather meant the hens were laying fewer eggs. It also meant they were more contrary about getting off their nests. But Meg had finished her thick mitt and kept it hidden behind the nesting boxes. Every morning she scattered the chicken feed, pulled on her mitt, and lifted those stubborn critters right off their nests. No more scars on her hands from the beaks of mean old hens. One time, she'd even used the mitt when she had to tackle Mr. Cock and put him where he belonged.

In the henhouse she fetched her thick mitt and was removing the contrary hens from their nests when Fred stepped inside the door.

"I've been wondering why you never complained about the old hens anymore," he said. "Now I know. You stole Mama's cloth scraps to make yourself a mitt."

"I wouldn't steal anything from Mama, Fred. You know that."

He stomped across the henhouse and grabbed the mitt from her hand. "We'll just see about this." Off he went toward the house.

Meg gathered the eggs, laid them carefully in the wicker basket, and followed her brother, wondering what Mama would have to say. By the time she came inside the warm kitchen, Mama was holding the mitt.

"What about this, Margaret? You took scraps without asking?"

Julia stopped setting the table and looked around. Papa had just entered the kitchen. Meg felt as though she were on display.

"Well?" Mama said.

Carefully, Meg explained how the idea came to her after being pecked so many times and after falling over the basket and breaking the eggs. "It was the bandage that first gave me the idea. I told Susannah about it and she offered to give me the scraps I needed."

"You asked the Hendrickses before you asked your mama?" Mama seemed almost hurt.

Meg was puzzled. She just supposed everyone would laugh at her idea if she had asked.

"I didn't ask her, Mama. I simply told Susannah my idea, and she offered."

Papa walked over to Mama's side. "Let's see that thing," he said. He took it, turned it over, and felt its thickness.

He smiled. "Have you been pecked since you've been wearing this?" he asked Meg.

"No, sir," she answered. "Not once."

"Seems like a pretty smart idea to me." He handed the mitt back to her. "Next time, though, ask your Mama first."

"Yes, sir," Meg answered. But she still wasn't sure Mama would have agreed. After all, Meg knew how picky Mama was about her scrap bag.

Fred's scowl never left his face all through breakfast. Meg wasn't sure if he were more upset over the elections or over not getting her in trouble about the mitt.

As she prepared to leave for school that morning, she had her completed sketch of Damon folded up and tucked inside her arithmetic book. Susannah was dying to see it.

Recently, she'd found it difficult to work on her sketches. Since the cold weather had set in, Meg felt tired much of the time and could barely stay awake after Julia fell asleep late at

93

night. But more than that, it was nearly impossible to make her fingers work in the cold, unheated upstairs bedroom.

Susannah was in awe of Meg's drawing when Meg showed it to her before school took up for the day. "It's so lifelike," she said. "You're a good artist, Meg. I just wish someone in your family could see it and help you."

Meg shook her head. "There's no sense wishing for what cannot be. If my mind dwelt on that, I'd be feeling sorry for myself all the time." Tucking the picture back into her book, she added, "I just try to be thankful for the little I can do. Perhaps one day it will be more."

Meg and Susannah told one another almost everything. When Susannah learned about Meg's secret trip to the art gallery, she was pleased. "I don't see how it can be wrong to follow your heart."

But Meg didn't tell her the part about seeing Damon in the garden, nor that he'd called out for her to stop. She couldn't bring herself to share that secret.

By the time school was out, Meg's nagging little headache was back. She couldn't wait to get home. She and Susannah were saying good-bye at the schoolyard gate when Fred came up behind Meg and bumped her on purpose. Her books and papers went flying all over the frozen snowy ground.

"Frederick Allerton!" Susannah cried. "You stop treating your sister like that."

"Aw, I didn't mean to. She was just in my way."

Meg stooped down to pick up her books and papers. Blowing up against the fence was her picture of Damon. Immediately Fred saw the sketch and grabbed it.

"Well, well, what's this? A picture of a boy. Meg's drawing pictures of boys," he taunted as he waved it in the air.

Julia had joined the group, and she wanted to see the picture. "Is that Meg's fella?"

Fred looked at the picture again. "Hey, I've seen him. He was at the institute. Meg's in love with the boy at the institute."

"Give me that," Meg pleaded. "Fred, that's mine. Give it back."

"Try and make me," he said. "Meggie's in love. Lovesick, lovesick Meggie," he jeered.

Just then Stephen came up from behind, grabbed Fred firmly by the arm, and snatched the picture away. "When are you ever going to learn to leave your sister alone?" Stephen said.

He looked at the drawing before handing it back to Meg. "Excellent drawing, Meg. What a splendid talent you have."

Meg gave a weak smile and thanked him. How she wished she could trade brothers with Susannah. She tucked the picture back into her book.

"I'm sorry," Susannah came up and whispered to her. "It was all because of me that you brought it."

"It's not your fault," Meg said. "But thank you anyway. Your encouragement helps so much."

Susannah and Stephen set out for the store, and the Allertons went down Liberty Street toward home. They hadn't gone far when up ahead they saw one of the sixth-grade boys teasing the German girls, Hulga and Ida.

"Here," Fred said to Julia, "take my book."

"Fred," Meg said, "where are you going?"

"He has no right to tease those girls."

Meg watched as Fred ran right up to the boy and demanded that he leave the girls alone. With the boy distracted, the two girls fled like frightened deer. But the boy got in a couple of good punches before Fred was able to break free. Then Fred ran as well.

Meg and Julia caught up with him a block or so from home. He'd ducked down a few alleys on the way. A cut above his eye was turning a nasty color.

"Fred, you know Mama doesn't want you picking a fight," Meg told him.

Fred dabbed at the cut with his handkerchief, then took his schoolbook from Julia. "That's all right," he said. "She doesn't want you drawing pictures, either. You don't tell, and I won't tell," he added smugly.

Meg could hardly believe his brazen attitude.

When they arrived home, Fred told Mama that a bigger boy had picked on him. Meg hated to hear him lie, but then she remembered that she hadn't told Mama the truth about the day Fred locked her out. It made her feel wretched. Would God forgive her for holding untruths in her heart?

When Papa came home and saw Fred's eye, he was more upset than Mama. "I want a son who will grow up to be temperate," he said firmly, "not a man who resorts to fisticuffs."

Although Fred didn't dare talk back, Meg knew her brother felt very strongly that what he'd done was right.

Meg didn't feel well that evening, but if she let up on her part of the work, Fred would accuse her of pretending to be sick. It was important that she not let anyone know how badly she felt.

After supper, during family prayers, Meg worried over the awful feelings she held in her heart against Fred. Why couldn't he see that he was no different than the boy who was teasing Hulga and Ida? Silently she prayed to be able to forgive Fred. But she also needed forgiveness. Confusion churned inside her.

The following Saturday night, the Allerton family gathered at the Hendrickses' home. As they sat around the heating stove in the elegant parlor, conversation ranged from the upcoming Thanksgiving holiday to the expected arrival of William Lloyd Garrison.

Uncle John reported that work had already begun on the free-labor store, and stock was arriving daily. People in the community were divided about the venture. Many opposed it, but a few seemed to welcome such a statement against slavery.

Meg sat with Susannah on the soft carpet near the stove. Both were working on their knitting, their needles making friendly clicking noises. The freestanding heating stove put out more heat than the fireplace in the Allertons' home. Waves of tiredness swept over Meg as the conversation droned about her and the heat from the stove made her drowsy.

As the men talked, Meg heard undercurrents of division between them. Papa felt that Mr. Garrison was far too radical. "He's hardhanded and bullheaded," Papa said. "That can cause hard feelings. People get hurt around Garrison. Not all antislavery thinkers agree with that man."

"Now, Ben," Uncle John argued, "if you'll remember correctly, ten years ago, no one was speaking out against slavery. It took a determined, single-minded man like Garrison to wake us up."

"Maybe so," Papa said. "But he still rubs me the wrong way."

Later, as the Allertons prepared to leave for home, Susannah asked if Meg could stay the night. Aunt Lucy quickly echoed the request. "Oh yes, Emma," Mama's friend said. "Could Meg stay? We'd love to have her."

Mama looked at Papa. Even though Meg and Susannah were close friends, they seldom stayed with one another. Mama always had work for Meg to do. To Meg's delight, Papa nodded.

"She doesn't have her church dress," Mama protested.

Aunt Lucy gave a wave of her hand. "It's so cold in church, she'll never unloose her cloak. No one will ever know the difference. And besides, the dress she has on is good enough for church."

"Very well, she may stay," Mama said.

Meg didn't care what she wore to church. She was just pleased to be able to stay around the Hendrickses. They always seemed so happy.

After the family had left, Aunt Lucy asked, "Would you girls like to sleep down here in the parlor on the floor?"

"Oh yes," Susannah said with a squeal. "What fun!"

They found an extra flannel nightgown for Meg, and then the three of them laughed and joked as Aunt Lucy helped the girls pile quilts on the parlor floor. After the makeshift bed was made, Aunt Lucy sat down in the midst of the blankets with the girls. She was in her gown and wrapper, and her long chestnut-colored hair was loosed and tied with a ribbon at the nape of her neck.

"Something tells me you aren't feeling well this evening," she said to Meg. "Is everything all right?"

Meg was surprised at Aunt Lucy's comment. How could she tell? Neither Mama nor Papa ever noticed. "It's nothing," she said. "I just get a little tired."

But Aunt Lucy persisted. "Tired like you're sleepy? Or tired like your body is weary?"

Again, Meg was amazed that her hostess could be so perceptive. "My whole body gets weary. Especially now in the cold weather." She rubbed at the back of her neck. "And it hurts a little right here."

"Turn around," Aunt Lucy said. "Let me give you a good neck rub."

Meg sat cross-legged as Aunt Lucy rubbed the tight muscles in her neck and shoulders.

"You're not exactly made like your mama," Aunt Lucy said.

"What do you mean?" Meg asked. She knew it was true, but it seemed so wrong to be so different.

"God made you like a delicate flower, while your mama is more like a strong oak tree."

Meg thought about that for a moment. "Won't I ever be a strong oak?"

"I highly doubt it. I've yet to see a flower grow into an oak. But I've seen many beautiful flowers in my day. And in God's plan, there is need for both."

Susannah was lying on her back, watching the two of them and listening.

"You're gentle and sensitive, Meg," Aunt Lucy went on. "Don't despise who you are. To the Lord you are like the bruised reed that He says He will not break."

"I know that verse," Susannah said. "It's in Isaiah."

"You mean it's all right that I'm not as strong as everyone else?" Meg asked quietly.

Suddenly a large log inside the stove settled with a soft

crunching noise, making them jump. Susannah giggled.

Aunt Lucy finished the neck rub, then put her arms about Meg and held her for a moment. "It's all right to be who you are. Period. Remember, Meg, there's more than one way to be strong. Now, if you have just a little bit of energy left, would you draw a picture for me?"

"You want me to draw for you?"

Aunt Lucy stood and went to the secretary in the corner of the parlor. "Mm-hm," she answered. "You don't mind, do you?"

Meg heard herself giggle. Right out loud, she giggled. What a wonderfully delightful question—to ask if she minded drawing a picture.

In just a few short minutes, she whipped out a light sketch of Susannah and her mother sitting on the blankets with their arms about one another's shoulders. They loved it.

Though Meg still felt achy in her joints, she was delirious with joy. She slept on the floor of the Hendrickses' parlor without waking once.

CHAPTER 12

Meeting Damon

Somehow things became a little easier for Meg after what Lucy told her. She still worked very hard. She still couldn't tell Mama how she felt, but it didn't bother her as much as it had before. No matter if she were carrying heavy buckets of hot water for the laundry, or scrubbing the floors, or mending Papa's heavy work trousers, she determined to keep up with Mama as best she could.

Lucy and John Hendricks had invited the Allertons to their home for a big Thanksgiving dinner, but Mama felt their family should be with Oma and Opa Schiller in Germantown. Meg was terribly disappointed. Thanksgiving didn't seem like Thanksgiving at Oma's house. Opa didn't like turkey. Instead they planned to roast a suckling pig.

Early that morning Meg and her family boarded the omnibus a few blocks from their house and rode the horse-drawn bus to Germantown. Each of them was laden down with a basket or parcel of some size. The driver spoke with an Irish brogue and wished them a happy Thanksgiving Day.

Meg hoped against hope that Papa would decide to stop by the Hendrickses' that evening. But nothing was said, and late that afternoon, they boarded another omnibus that took them straight home. Although Meg tried to be thankful, she felt it had been a rather dreary Thanksgiving.

On a cold night early in December, Meg was sitting next to Papa in the front room, knitting another pair of woolen stockings for Fred. He seemed to wear his out almost as quickly as she and Mama could knit them. Mama had gone to fetch more yarn, Julia was in the kitchen, and Fred was out splitting kindling.

Papa had unfolded his newspaper and sat quietly reading. After a moment or two, he mumbled something under his breath. Meg could have sworn she heard the name "Damon."

"What did you say, Papa?" she asked softly.

"Oh nothing. Just an article here in the paper."

"What does the article say?"

"Odd name, Damon Pollard. It says here that the young child prodigy, Damon Pollard, has been brought to Cincinnati by his uncle, John P. Foote, president of the Ohio Mechanics Institute, to study under the famous black artist, Robert Scott Duncanson. There'll be a special showing at the institute beginning this week, featuring this young man's art."

Meg's breath caught in her throat. Nephew of President

Foote. Child prodigy. Damon truly was a special person. Somehow she'd known it all along.

Papa read a little further. "What do you know about this? His parents died of yellow fever." More softly, her father added, "Just like my mother and father died."

Meg's mind was spinning. How long would the showing of Damon's work be held? A few days? A few weeks? She had to see his work. But how? And what if she missed the showing altogether?

The next day she shared her newest secret with Susannah. Susannah's eyes grew wide. "So he's President Foote's nephew, is he? That means he must live on the grounds."

"I wonder what it would be like to be at the institute every day, walking among all the wonderful paintings," Meg said.

"Will you try to go see his showing?"

Meg shook her head. "I don't see how I can."

The two were standing out in the cold, waiting for one of the teachers to clang the morning bell.

"Won't your mama be sending you to see your Oma?"

"We don't go as often in winter. Only if the day breaks clear."

"Well, that's simple then. We'll just pray for clearing weather."

Meg wasn't even sure if she should pray about going to see Damon Pollard's art showing. It was frightening to think of doing something without Mama's knowledge.

Amazingly, the next Saturday dawned as clear and sunny as a spring day. Of course it was sharply cold, but it was clear. Fred went off with Papa, and then Mama decided that

Meg should walk to Oma's. Meg could scarcely believe what she was hearing.

Had the Lord answered Susannah's prayer?

Mama even allowed Meg to leave just before lunchtime so she could come back before dark. Julia complained that she wanted to go as well. Meg held her breath as Mama paused before answering her little sister's pleas. Finally Mama said, "Margaret and Frederick were both nine before walking to Oma's was allowed for them. You must wait your turn."

Though Julia wasn't pleased, she held her peace.

"If you don't send me with a basket," Meg suggested, "perhaps Oma won't think she must fill it for my return trip." Meg didn't relish coming home with a heavy basket on her arm.

Mama nodded. "It may be you are right." She took a loaf of her *Hefekuchen*, a sweet bread, and wrapped it in brown paper. "There," she said. "That will suffice."

Meg hurriedly put on her bonnet and warm cloak before Mama could think of anything else. She did remember to put a woolen muffler about her neck. Then she took off.

The canal was frozen. No boats moved during the winter. In some areas, the ice was swept clear of snow so young people could skate. Meg quickly made her way across the bridge and down past the German shops to Oma's house.

Oma was surprised to see her granddaughter on a cold December day. Meg found it difficult to concentrate on their conversation as she kept thinking about going to the institute. Could she really go? Was she borrowing trouble, as Mama would say? But if she didn't go this day, there might never be another opportunity.

Oma served large helpings of apple streudel drowned in

cream. Meg could not eat all hers, and Oma commented on how thin she was. "That mama of yours, she is feeding you enough? A mere skin and bones you are."

"I don't need much to eat," Meg told her.

"At Thanksgiving dinner I watched. You did not eat much." Oma finished off her streudel and added, "Never heard of a Schiller with no appetite."

Meg was tempted to remind Oma her name was Allerton, but she didn't want to be unkind.

By midafternoon, the skies grew overcast. "Was too good to last," Oma said. "Best that you hurry on home now. The weather, it can turn nasty in minutes."

If anything, Meg was thankful for the low gray clouds that set her on her way earlier. Now she had even more time before dark. Surely this was an answer to prayer as well.

Oma sent her home with a round of cheese. It was somewhat heavier than the bread, but at least it wasn't a basketful of goodies.

As she had done a few weeks earlier, Meg turned south toward the institute, rather than west toward home. The clouds had rolled in quickly, and even before she crossed the canal bridge, tiny flakes of snow began to fall.

By the time she reached the massive stone building, Meg was wet and cold. It took all her strength to push open the tall wooden door. The caretaker came out from the anteroom.

"Well now, miss. You're out in rather nasty weather."

"Please," she said, "tell me where I can find the showing for Damon Pollard."

"It's on the third floor gallery," he said. "You'll see the signs at the top of the stairs."

"Thank you very much," Meg said, quite out of breath.

Up the stairs she went, pausing at each landing to catch her breath. It was snowing harder now. She must hurry.

The signs on wrought iron stands pointed the way to the correct gallery. Suddenly, she was in the midst of work all done by a young man perhaps the age of Stephen. Meg found that difficult to believe.

Meg had the room all to herself. Slowly she made one sweep around the room, looking closely at every work. Some were landscapes. There were a few still lifes. One or two portraits. Mostly landscapes. Mostly oils.

Though she did not have the eye of an expert, Meg felt the paintings were very good. How fortunate Damon was to have an uncle who cared about his work and supported and encouraged him. If only she had someone to teach her. Her simple sketches paled in comparison to these works.

Suddenly a voice at the door said, "I thought you might come."

Startled, Meg gasped and whirled about. There was Damon Pollard leaning against the doorpost, his dark eyes twinkling. Her hand flew to her face and she nearly dropped the cheese.

He stepped toward her, and she drew back. "I didn't intend to frighten you," he said softly. "Please don't run away." He waved his hand about the room. "Do you like what you see?"

She nodded, unable to speak.

"I saw you when you came with the Liberty School group. You like art. I could tell. You took more interest in the paintings than the rest of the students."

He couldn't have seen her. It was impossible. Her mind wouldn't let her believe it.

"Then you came alone. I saw you from the garden, and I called to you, but you ran off."

"I must go," she said. "I'm not even supposed to be here." She stepped toward the door, but he was filling it.

"You snuck away to come and see my work? Now I *am* flattered." He looked at her cloak. "Your wrap is wet from the snow. Won't you come to my uncle's cottage to dry off?"

She shook her head. "Please let me by. I must go."

"You can't go back out in that snow."

"I don't live far away."

"I will step from the doorway and let you pass by only if you will tell me your name."

Meg's heart was pounding. "My name is Meg. Now please, I must be going."

"Meg? Short for Margaret?"

She nodded. Though she longed to look at him and study the dark eyes and chiseled features, she kept her eyes to the floor. Presently, he stepped aside.

"Wait until I get my cloak," he said. "I'll see you safely home."

"No! Please!" Now that she was in the hallway, she ran. She ran down all three flights and ran out the front door into the blinding snow. The wind and the cold struck her in the face and seemed to suck the breath right out of her.

How foolish she'd been. Never had she ever been so ashamed of herself. With her head down, bending into the wind, Meg trudged through the deepening snow toward home.

CHAPTER 13

Lost in the Blizzard

Meg pushed her way through nearly deserted streets. She knew she should stop somewhere and get warm. But what would Mama say? Meg wasn't even supposed to be in this area south of their neighborhood. She should have gone straight home from Oma's. If she had, she would have stayed dry and warm.

With each block it became harder for Meg to see through the blinding snow, but she pressed on. At one point, she stepped into the doorway of a church just to get out of the wind for a moment. She had to keep going. The hood of her cloak was pulled up over her bonnet, but the wind pierced through as though she wore no wrap at all.

Just when she thought she couldn't take another step, she

saw the corner of John and Everett Streets. Her own neighborhood. Just a few more blocks. Her head was swimming. Every house looked the same. The snow was so thick she could barely see the houses. She thought she'd crossed two streets. That meant her house was the third one on the left. It took all her strength to lift the latch on the gate and struggle up the front walk. She made an attempt to climb the front steps, but then collapsed on the porch.

Meg awakened in the parlor of a strange house. Standing over her was Mrs. Wirth, their neighbor. Meg hadn't made it to her house after all. She was lying on a davenport with a quilt over her. Though she felt warm once again, shivers kept coursing through her.

"Ah, you've come around. Poor little thing. Out in this frightful blizzard. It's a wonder you made it at all."

Meg's fingers and toes stung like fire. She tried to lift her head. "How long have I been here? Mama will be worried."

"Now, now. Just rest easy. You've only been here a short while. Mr. Wirth went to tell your family you're safe."

"I couldn't see. Snow was so thick."

"Lie back and don't try to talk. I'm making you a little broth to warm your insides."

"I need to get home," Meg said.

"Now why go home? You're safe and warm right here. No sense going back out in that frightful storm. It'll let up directly, and then your papa can come get you." Mrs. Wirth moved to the door of the parlor. "I'll get your broth."

The beef broth that Mrs. Wirth fed her was tasty and warm. Meg wanted to say she could feed herself, but she didn't want to hurt Mrs. Wirth's feelings. The broth was followed by a cup of hot, strong tea.

"Now you can lie back and sleep a spell," Mrs. Wirth told her.

"I'm sorry to have caused so much trouble," Meg said.

"What trouble? To give you a bit of broth and a cup of tea? I'm more than happy that you made it to our doorstep."

Just then they heard the sound of the front door opening. Mr. Wirth had returned. Mr. Wirth was a big man with a quick wit and a ready laugh. After he had shaken the snow off his clothes, he came into the parlor.

"Your family's mighty glad to hear you're faring well. Your papa will be down to fetch you home when the storm breaks. That might not be till morning."

"I'm sorry to be putting you out like this, Mr. Wirth," Meg said.

"Glad to do it, little one. Glad to do it." He stepped to the fire and warmed his hands. "They sent your little brother out to find you, but he couldn't see any trace of you. They thought sure you was a goner."

Meg shriveled inside. Of course Fred couldn't find her. He didn't know what direction she was coming from.

"He probably set out after you came in here," Mrs. Wirth put in. "Chances are you just missed one another."

Meg had never felt so miserable. What if Fred had been lost in the blizzard because of her? The guilt was almost more than she could bear.

Meg spent the night in the Wirths' parlor, sleeping fitfully. She dreamed of Fred lost in the blizzard and sounds of Damon calling her to come and look at his paintings.

The next morning, sleigh bells filled the crisp morning air as people hitched up their sleighs to go to church. Meg threw back the quilt and attempted to stand. Her shoes and

110

stockings were sitting by the hearth. She walked to fetch them, and while her toes hurt some, they felt much better than they had the night before. She supposed Mama and Papa would forego church in this weather.

Meg could smell breakfast cooking in the kitchen. After putting on her shoes and stockings, she made her way to the kitchen, where Mrs. Wirth was working. Mr. Wirth was sitting at the table. Both seemed pleased that she was up and about.

"I'm sure your papa will be here shortly," he said. "Please sit and eat with us."

Mrs. Wirth took her to a back bedroom, where Meg washed up and rebraided her hair. Then she ate a good helping of steak and eggs. Just as they were finishing, Papa came knocking on the back door. Meg jumped up and ran to hug him. To her surprise, he returned her hug.

"Hey there, Meggie," he said. "You had us pretty worried yesterday. That storm came in quicker than anything I've seen in a long time."

She nodded. She didn't really want to talk about it. "I'll get my cloak, Papa."

The cloak, too, had been spread out in the parlor to dry. She put it on along with her bonnet and was ready to go. But the cheese. Where was Oma's cheese?

"Mrs. Wirth," Meg said. "Did I have a package with me when you found me?"

"No package, Meg, but it could be out in the snow."

"Oma sent a round of cheese with me, Papa."

Papa smiled. "No time to be concerned about a round of cheese. Come on. Let's get you home."

And with that, Papa lifted her right up in his arms and

carried her all the way home through the snow, just like a hero in a storybook. It made her feel very special.

Fred was quite miffed because of all the attention Meg was receiving. "When you saw the storm coming," he said, "you should have just stayed at Oma's. That's what you should have done, you silly goose."

But Papa made him shush. "It's all over now, Frederick. I'll have no more talk about what should or should not have been done."

Mama fussed over Meg, looking at her fingers and toes to make sure they were not frostbitten. Then she said, "So sorry I am that I sent you, Margaret. This time of year, I should not have taken the chance."

"Papa said not to talk of what should have been done, Mama. I'm all right. That's what matters."

That night Meg curled up beside Julia in her own featherbed piled heavy with down-filled quilts. She thought about the past two days and how she'd upset the entire household because of her foolishness. Silently, she prayed for God to forgive her.

But before she fell asleep, she once again remembered the wonderful paintings of Damon Pollard. He was indeed a talented young man. She couldn't honestly say she was sorry she'd seen his work. So did that mean her repentance wasn't genuine? It was so confusing. How could her thoughts be so muddled?

The next morning there were no eggs to gather, but Meg still had to feed the chickens. Papa had cleared a path to the chicken house and a spot in the chicken pen. Meg filled the pans with feed and scattered it, calling for the chickens to come. Every movement made her so very tired.

The walk to school, trudging through deep snow, wore her out, and during class time she could barely hold her head up. At recess Susannah was excited that there was going to be a snowball fight. But Meg said she'd better stay in. Susannah gave her a worried look. "Are you feeling all right?"

"I'm all right. I just don't think I need to take any chances. I'm still a little weak."

Susannah nodded. "Then I'll ask if I can stay in with you."

After receiving permission, the two girls sat at Susannah's desk in the fifth-grade room and talked, while Meg sketched pictures in her friend's copybook.

At noon the students ate lunch at their desks. Meg didn't feel like eating.

Throughout the afternoon, it seemed that Mrs. Gravitt kept looking right at Meg. She called on her several times, during history and again during language. It took all Meg's energy and concentration to keep from putting her head on her desk and falling asleep.

Thankfully, men who worked for the city had been out during the day with shovels. By the time they walked home, a few paths had been cleared. Fred and Julia kept up a line of chatter as they walked along, but Meg barely listened. She felt as though weights had been tied to her feet. It was a struggle just to put one foot in front of the other.

That night, before Papa came home to supper, Mama had the flatirons heating on the stove and the board up in a corner of the kitchen. She had dried the wash in front of the kitchen stove and now there was ironing to do. Meg was expected to do her share. When Meg had finished only a few pieces, Mama asked her what the matter was.

"I'm still a little tired from Saturday, I suppose," she answered.

"I suppose you're going to use that excuse forever," Fred piped up. "You were in the snow for only a little while. You act like it was some big calamity."

Mama came over to her and felt her forehead. "Mm. No fever."

Meg could have told her there was no fever. She did feel too warm though—probably from the ironing.

When Papa came in that night, he was carrying the round of cheese from Oma. Mrs. Wirt had found it in the snow near her front gate, right where Meg had dropped it.

Meg knew there would be no sketching that night. She could hardly wait for bedtime so she could rest her aching body. Her head nodded as Papa read Scripture. Papa said she should pay attention when God's Word was read. Mama just shook her head. Meg wondered what it would be like to be strong like Mama.

Morning came much too quickly. Meg lay in bed and felt as though she could sleep forever and still never be fully rested. On her feet was the warm weight of Goldie sleeping peacefully, which made it even more difficult to get up. She forced herself up out of the warm covers and onto the cold floor. "Come on, Julia," she said. "Time to get up."

From beneath the quilts, Julia groaned, "I don't want to get up."

"It doesn't matter. We must get up."

Meg broke the thin layer of ice in the pitcher and poured water into the basin. Quickly she washed her face and hands before changing into her school dress with warm under-things and woolen petticoats beneath. Goldie jumped up on the washstand and lapped noisily at the water in the basin.

Again she woke Julia and brought her younger sister's dress to her so she could get ready for school. By the time Meg was ready to go downstairs, Julia was finally out of the bed.

"Don't forget to make the bed," Meg reminded her. At least Mama was finally assigning Julia a few jobs.

"I won't forget," Julia answered in a sour tone.

Meg hurried down the steps with Goldie right behind her. After the chickens were fed, Meg was slowly walking back to the porch when Fred called out from the woodpile. "You still trying to make everyone feel sorry for you? Well, your act's wasted on me."

Meg took hold of the porch post to pull herself up the steps. For once, she didn't care what Fred said. She didn't even try to answer. Inside, she hung up her cloak and gave Mama a hand with breakfast. Then she sat down beside Papa to eat. Frederick was loading wood in Mama's cookstove.

Suddenly it was as though Mama had turned down the coal oil lamp. Everything was dark, and Meg felt herself slipping from her chair onto the floor. She was helpless to stop the fall.

CHAPTER 14
The Doctor's Plan

As though through a fog, Meg heard Fred saying, "Aw, she's just puttin' on, Mama. You know how she can act. It's just a show so she can get out of work."

Papa was shushing him, then Meg heard the word "doctor." She tried to open her eyes. She was lying on the horse-hair davenport in the front room. Mama was kneeling beside her. Papa was standing over her, and a frightened Julia peeked around from behind Papa.

"I'll be all right," Meg said weakly.

"We'll see," Papa said. "Dr. Logan will tell us for sure."

Fred and Julia got ready to leave for school, and Papa left

to go fetch the doctor. Once they were gone and she could hear sounds of Mama working to clean up breakfast, Meg slipped into a delicious sleep, only to be awakened later by Papa returning with Dr. Logan.

The last time Dr. Logan had been in their home was when Julia was born. Meg had been only five, but she could remember the old gray-haired doctor. He'd come down the stairs and announced that Mama had had a little girl. Then Papa'd fixed the doctor a mug of coffee before he left. Meg recalled how excited she'd been over having a sister.

Now the doctor was back again for no real reason. He checked Meg over and made a few sounds like "Hm" and "Uh huh" but said very little. Then she heard him talking to Mama and Papa in a soft voice in the front hall. Finally he was gone, and she was able to sleep again.

Once or twice Mama tried to get her to take some broth, but she could hardly lift her head to do so. All she wanted to do was sleep. Sometime during the day, Mama helped her out of her school dress and into her flannel gown. Goldie stayed snuggled up close to Meg.

That afternoon when Fred and Julia came home, Fred said, "Well, well, the lazybones is still lazing about. That Margaret gets away with everything."

"Frederick Allerton, you hush up right this minute," Meg heard Julia reply. "Meg is real sick, and you act like you don't even care."

Meg could hardly believe her ears—Julia standing up to her older brother? But Meg's brain was too foggy to even thank Julia for her words, and Meg soon settled back to sleep.

The days melted together in a soft blur. Meg wasn't sure

when one day ended and the next one began. Sometimes she'd hear sounds from the kitchen, and she knew she should be in there helping. Who was feeding the chickens? Would the chickens starve because she was shirking her work? She never went upstairs to bed, but was allowed to sleep in the front room instead.

One morning Meg woke up and wondered why she wasn't getting any better. She felt she should at least get up and try to walk around. Just then Mama came in the room.

"You are finally awake?"

"May I get up now?" Meg asked.

Mama shook her head. "Doctor says to be in bed for a time will help you get well."

"What do I have?"

Again Mama shook her head. "He does not know. Just that you are weak and need rest, he says."

"But I need to help with the work. And what about school?"

"Susannah will bring your books this afternoon. She brings assignments from your instructor as well."

Meg would be glad to see Susannah. As much as she needed her rest, she wanted to be up and about. "May I come to the table to eat?"

"Tomorrow perhaps. We'll see."

That afternoon, Susannah fairly burst into the Allertons' front room. "Oh, Meg," Susannah gushed. "I've missed you terribly. I don't even like school when you're not there."

Julia and Fred had followed Susannah into the front room, but now Mama came and shooed them out. "Let Meg and Susannah visit," she said firmly.

Susannah put down the books in her arms, took off her cloak, and pulled a chair over near the sofa. "Do you feel terribly bad? Julia told us you were awful sick."

"I don't feel badly," Meg told her. "Just very tired."

"Well, I have exciting news that will make you feel better." She scooted the chair a little closer and lowered her voice. "There's to be a city-wide art contest for all the schools. It's sponsored by the institute. President Foote himself is going around to all the schools to announce it."

"President Foote came to our school?"

Susannah nodded and smiled. "See there? I knew you'd be excited. There'll be different categories for different age groups. Oh Meg, you just *have* to enter. No matter what anyone says, your art should be important. I don't know why you don't stand up for what you believe in."

All Susannah's words were making Meg weary. It required too much strength to think. "I don't know—"

"It's not right now. I didn't mean for you to jump up and start drawing now. The contest will be in the spring. And the winner will be part of a special showing at the institute at the close of the school year. Isn't that wonderful?"

Meg allowed herself to imagine for a moment what that might be like. But then she could imagine Mama solemnly shaking her head and Fred taunting. "Perhaps by spring I'll feel better," she said, hoping Susannah would drop the subject. "What work did Mrs. Gravitt send?" she asked.

"Plenty of hard work. I hope by next year Mrs. Gravitt either changes schools, changes classrooms, or quits teaching."

Meg smiled. "I think there is little chance of any of those happening." Then she added, "She's not so bad, Susannah. Just a little strict."

"After all those sentences she made you write? And you still say nice things about her?" Susannah shook her head in disbelief. She pulled out a paper on which Mrs. Gravitt had written the assignments and handed it to Meg. At the bottom of the page, in swirling penmanship, Mrs. Gravitt had added a nice note wishing Meg a quick recovery.

As Susannah rose to go, she said, "We're beginning to decorate the rooms for Christmas. Our class made paper candles today and put them in each window."

Christmas. Meg could hardly believe it.

"You just have to be better by Christmas," Susannah added as she put on her cloak and prepared to leave.

Meg wanted to agree, but how could she be sure? She still didn't know what the doctor had said. "Thank you so much for bringing my books."

"Oh, I wanted to," Susannah said. "I've missed you so. I asked Mama if I could come over on Saturday to see you again. She said I may."

Suddenly the awful weariness swept over Meg again. If company wore her out that much, she wasn't sure a long visit would be good, but she hesitated to say so.

The days that followed were filled with frustration and boredom. Meg could only do her schoolwork for short periods of time before the weariness took over. But she kept on trying. Julia was kind enough to take her papers and turn them in.

Some days Meg felt a little better, and she thought surely she was on the mend. Then there would be a setback.

On Christmas Day, she was allowed to go with the family to the Hendrickses'. It was the first time she'd been out since the day she'd fainted at the breakfast table.

At midmorning, Uncle John and Stephen came to take them all in the sleigh. Mama bundled Meg up as though she were a tiny baby. It felt good to be outside once again. The sharp, cold air was tingly on Meg's face. Bright sunshine sparkled on the fresh new snow, and everyone was laughing and calling out "Merry Christmas" to one another.

The sleigh bells jingled and the runners gave off a humming sound as they skimmed over the snowy streets. Bare trees cast lacy shadows here and there on the pure white snow. Since it was only a few blocks from the Allerton house to the Hendrickses', Uncle John decided to take them for a ride about town "just for the fun of it," he said. How wonderful to do something just for the fun of it. Meg wished her family would do something just for fun.

Though she still had very little appetite, just the aromas of the magnificent Christmas dinner gave Meg great joy. She took a small helping of almost everything on the table, including the pumpkin pie. Mama made her lie down and rest in the afternoon, which seemed odd. Never before had Meg been so fussed over. She could tell it still irritated Fred. He continued to accuse her of pretending, though not as often as before.

Late in the afternoon, Meg walked into the kitchen and heard Mama saying something to Aunt Lucy about Yellow Springs. Meg knew of only one place by that name. It was a health resort near Dayton where rich people went. As Meg entered the room, Mama hushed. But Aunt Lucy said, "I think you should talk to Meg about it."

"Talk to me about what?" Meg asked.

Mama's face looked troubled.

"She'll have to know sooner or later," Aunt Lucy insisted.

Mama pulled out a chair for Meg and then sat down with her at the table. "The doctor, he says you need time away to get your strength back. He says good things happen to sick

121

people at Yellow Springs because of the mineral water there. A place where you can get better. But all of us cannot go." Her Mama gave a shrug.

"So," Aunt Lucy said, "I was suggesting that your Oma could take you. It would be good for her to get away as well."

"Take me?" Meg's weary head was spinning again. None of this made any sense. She'd never gone anywhere before without Mama and Papa.

"You could take a canal boat to Dayton, then take the stage to Yellow Springs," Aunt Lucy explained.

"The canal is frozen," Meg put in. At least her mind could say that much.

Aunt Lucy laughed. "In the spring, Meg. We're talking about when the weather breaks and the boats are running again."

"Won't I be well before then?" The thought of being sick the rest of the winter was almost more than Meg could bear.

Aunt Lucy put her arm about Meg's shoulders. "You will be well again, but it's going to take time."

Meg looked over at Mama. "Do you want me to go to Yellow Springs?"

Mama glanced down at her hands folded in her lap. "Your papa and I want you to be well. We will do what the doctor says."

Meg's sickness had caused enough trouble as it was. Such a trip would cost her parents a great deal of money. She'd be taking a trip with Oma, and she didn't even like to be with her grandmother more than one afternoon at a time. How would she manage this?

If she'd not stopped by the institute that afternoon in the snowstorm, she never would have gotten sick at all. Meg felt weighted down by guilt.

CHAPTER 15
To Yellow Springs

By February, Meg returned to school for two or three days a week. She wasn't allowed to go out for recess, even on the sunniest days. She was still behind on some of her lessons.

When Fred learned about her upcoming trip, he acted as though Meg had planned the whole thing. As they walked back and forth to school, he complained about the unfairness of it all. "I've always wanted to ride a canal boat," he told her. "Why should you get to go just because you're a little bit sick?"

Julia had ceased to side with Fred. This, too, was a frustration for Fred, and he turned to picking on Julia. Julia, however, stood up to him. "You should be praying for Meg to get well," Julia would say to her brother, "instead of talking so mean all the time."

Since Meg no longer had to stay in bed, the days passed more quickly. Mama purchased fabric at the mercantile and sewed Meg two new dresses to wear on the trip. Meg was thankful since she knew other ladies and girls staying at Yellow Springs would be dressed in fine fashions. However, what she would do with two new dresses after the trip, Meg couldn't imagine.

One morning at school, Susannah asked Meg about the art contest. "Have you thought any more about entering?" she wanted to know.

The mention of the contest irritated Meg. "Susannah, I've been sick. Mama and Papa have told me not to waste time sketching. Now just how do you think I would ever be able to enter a contest?"

Meg had never spoken a cross word to her dearest friend, and the moment the words were out, she felt terrible. But Susannah just laughed.

"I thought you'd never ask," she said. "You can draw all you please during your time away."

Her words caught Meg by surprise. The thought had never occurred to her.

"Just think about it," Susannah continued, "perhaps the opportunity will present itself."

The canal opened the first week in March, and Oma and Meg had their tickets to ride to Dayton. The docking area was filled with the bustle of a busy commerce area. Freight packets were loading and unloading.

High-pitched horns sounded to signal an approaching boat, and the captains called out to hail one another as they passed in the shallow canal. Wheels clattered over the cobblestones as carriages, wagons, and drays crowded about to take care of business and deliver passengers.

Meg's plump, happy-faced Opa was there to see them off, as was her family and the four Hendrickses. Meg felt almost elegant in her new blue silk dress covered with flounces and ruffles.

Since some of Meg's strength had returned, she argued that this trip was a waste of money, but Mama and Papa insisted that she go. So here she was.

Fred insisted he'd rather ride the train than a canal boat any day. After Meg had hugged everyone—except Fred, who would only allow a handshake—Susannah stepped forward with a brown package in her hands. "We have a going-away gift for you," she said. "You can open it on the way. It's a surprise."

Everyone began talking at once. The captain stood on the bow of the boat and blew his horn. Meg was surprised to see that Mama had tears in her eyes. Within a few minutes, the boat was moving, towed by the mules who walked on the path along the canal. Meg looked back to see everyone waving and Mama dabbing her eyes. Fred's hands were in his pockets.

At first, Meg had a strange sensation in her stomach at leaving everyone behind. She wasn't sure if it was fear or excitement. She and Oma went inside the spacious cabin to see the area where they would eat and sleep.

Several men had already set up a backgammon board and a lively game was underway. Meg had heard stories of boat rides on crowded packets where the owners oversold the space and there was barely room to sleep or eat. Thankfully

125

that wasn't the case on this trip.

Since the day was clear, she and Oma went up the stairs to the roof, where chairs and benches were arranged for them to sit. Once they were out of the city, which took a couple hours, the countryside was peaceful. There were few noises other than the lapping of water at the sides of the canal and the clip-clop of mules' feet on the towpath.

Meg had heard that on the Erie Canal in New York, the bridges across the canal were built low and nearly scraped passengers off the boats. But on the Miami, nice hump-backed bridges were built, and the roof-riders had no fears of being knocked off.

Farther out into the rural areas, people would congregate on the bridges. Some sold vegetables and fresh eggs to the packet cook. Others called out the names of their taverns, encouraging debarking passengers to come and stay. Still others asked for news because the canal was their link to the big city of Cincinnati.

After a few hours, Oma became weary and Meg escorted her down the steps into the cabin, where she could sit in a more comfortable chair and rest. It was only then that Meg remembered her going-away gift. Hurrying back to the roof, she took the package from her valise and untied the string. Two well-dressed ladies with ruffled parasols looked on.

"Your birthday?" one asked.

Meg looked up at her. "No, ma'am. A going-away gift from my friends."

The paper fell open and she let out a little gasp, which made the ladies twitter. Meg should have guessed. There was a box of colored pencils, a box of charcoals, and a small sketch pad—just the right size for holding in her lap.

She had all the time in the world, and Oma was resting. Eagerly, Meg opened the sketch pad and began to sketch.

Meg didn't actually try to hide her work from Oma, but she was still guarded. After all, Oma would be talking to Mama later on. Why take a chance of being reprimanded? So when Oma returned to the roof, Meg put the work back in her valise and pulled out her embroidery.

As they chatted, Oma recalled when she and Opa Walford had left the beautiful Black Forest of Germany and traveled across the Atlantic Ocean to the United States.

"Not quiet like this, it was," she said. "Rocking, pitching about. People terrible sick. But," she added, "safe we docked in New York Harbor. That is all that matters."

Following a fine supper, a crimson curtain was strung across the cabin. The women were bedded down in the front half, while the men stayed in the back half of the boat. Women releasing bustles and stepping out of hoops and rustling crinolines created an interesting commotion. Seeing the narrow berths that folded down from the walls, Meg was immediately thankful for her small size. Oma had quite a time getting her stout frame in any sort of comfortable position.

But even though she fit in the small berth, Meg had a hard time sleeping. Through the curtain came the heavy sounds of men snoring.

By the time they arrived in Dayton the next afternoon, Meg had completed several sketches and felt rested. At Dayton, they disembarked and were taken to the Midland Tavern. There they waited for the stage bound for Yellow Springs to arrive.

Compared to the quiet ride of the canal packet, the stage was loud, rowdy, and dusty. Meg feared that Oma would be quite shaken to pieces on the rough ride.

Leather curtains, which were snapped down in foul weather, were rolled up, letting the dust blow freely through the coach. Oma covered her mouth with her hankie and coughed. Meg wasn't sure if it was due to the dust or the cigar smoke from a well-dressed gentleman with a shiny gold watch fob.

Meg fairly flew from her seat when the stage hit the deepest bumps on the rutted road. Hanging on for dear life didn't help much. The way grew steeper as they entered into hilly country. At one point the driver ordered all passengers out to lighten the load as the stage made its way to the top of the tree-studded ridge. All but Oma, that is. The driver said she should ride. Meg and Oma both thanked him for the kindness.

Though Meg's new dress was becoming quite dusty, still she was excited by all the goings-on. But for Oma's sake, she was thankful when late that afternoon the driver called out, "Yellow Springs just ahead."

Meg had heard stories about the discovery of the mineral springs and how a resort had become highly popular among the monied folk. She wasn't sure what she expected to see, but it was nothing like what came into view. After she allowed the driver to assist her down from the stage, she gazed up at the massive stone structure tucked away behind a curtain of dense trees.

The serene beauty nearly took her breath away. Flagstone pathways with wooden railings curved through the trees up to the lodge. A wide veranda wrapped around the front of the lodge, trimmed out in elegant stone arches. Through the arched openings in the veranda, Meg could see a number of white rocking chairs. She was sure she was going to love this beautiful place.

CHAPTER 16

The Surprise Guest

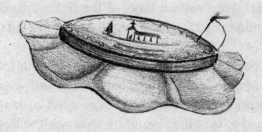

Courteous stewards assisted with the baggage and led Meg and Oma through the trees and up the walk. Meg was gawking about so much, she nearly stumbled on the small stone steps that led up to the lodge.

As she climbed the steps, she could see that the veranda was much wider than it appeared from the bottom of the hill. The rustic lobby was set about with comfortable rough-wood furniture and bearskin rugs on the gray slate floors. One wall housed a mammoth stone fireplace.

Their second-story room was open and airy with a view of the wooded hills and valleys that lay before them in a sunny haze. Meg stood staring out the bay window, hardly able to take her eyes from the magnificent scenery.

Though Meg didn't feel weary, Oma insisted she lie down and rest. Oma removed her veiled travel bonnet and her gloves, and stretched out in the upholstered chaise. Within moments, the elderly traveler was sound asleep. Meg took her art supplies out of the valise, quietly opened the door, and escaped to the veranda, where she spent the better part of the afternoon.

Yellow Springs Resort believed in healthy foods—mostly fruits and vegetables, very little meat, and plenty of good cold spring water. After several days of the healthy food and the refreshing mineral baths, Meg began to feel like a brand new person.

At the end of the first week, she received a letter from Susannah. Meg tore away the wax seal and unfolded the letter. Her friend reported that Fred was upset over news that Congress had passed the resolution to annex the Republic of Texas.

"That, plus the fact that he never wanted Polk as president, has the boy in a dither," Susannah wrote. Then she went on to explain how they'd given a tea for William Lloyd Garrison at their home, but Meg's mama and papa failed to show up.

There was that sleeping sawyer that Meg had been so worried about. She wondered how Papa's decision had affected her brother. Susannah's letter continued:

Mr. Garrison is a fascinating man, full of passion and incredibly focused on one goal: to abolish slavery in our country forever. When I hear him talk, I fairly believe it could happen. His eyes spit fire when he talks of his dreams, but otherwise he is kind and gentle and extremely mannerly. I do hope Fred can meet him before he leaves. The free-labor store is nearly ready to open, after which Mr. Garrison will depart Cincinnati.

At Oma's request, Meg read some of the letter aloud, but Oma cared little about politics or the issues of slavery. When Meg finished reading, Oma said, "But nothing she says about my Emma. How is der family?"

"I'm sure if they were not fine, Susannah would have told us," Meg assured her, tucking the letter back into her bag.

As they sat together on the veranda, a soft spring breeze wafted in from out of the wooded hills. Meg felt as though her lungs could never drink in enough of the sweet, clear air.

The air in the city never smelled so good. What with the filth in the streets, smoke from the foundries, and smells from the packing houses, the air in Cincinnati left much to be desired.

As it did every afternoon, the stage pulled up at the bottom of the hill to unload the passengers. Meg enjoyed watching the well-dressed guests leaving and arriving. She craned her neck to catch a glimpse. As a tall, slender figure stepped down off the step of the stage with a little bounce, Meg gasped and accidentally stabbed her finger with her embroidery needle. "Ow," she cried.

"Careful you must be," Oma warned her. "A spot of blood might set in the linen and never come out."

No, no, Meg's mind was crying. *It can't be.* But there he was, standing tall and serene, looking about him, and breathing deeply of the fresh air: Damon Pollard.

She had to get out of there. Quickly. What if he saw her

with her German Oma? He'd know Meg couldn't really afford to be at the resort. She didn't belong in this elegant place with all its lavish provisions.

"My pricked finger is bleeding," Meg told Oma. "I'll go take care of it with cold water."

Lodge stewards were hurrying down the steps to meet the new guests. Meg picked up all her work, shoved it into her bag, and stood to her feet. "You needn't come, Oma. I'll return later—if I feel like it."

Oma looked up now. "You feel poorly once again?"

Meg put her hand to her forehead. "A little. I'm not sure. I'll tell you later."

The guests were starting up the steps. Meg ran inside and up the stairs to her room as quickly as she could and collapsed into a chair, her heart pounding. Whatever would she do?

"I believe I'll not go down to eat this evening," she told Oma when her grandmother came to check on her.

"It is a setback you have." Oma felt Meg's forehead. "Mm. A little warm, as I thought. Lie down. Rest. Mineral water, perhaps it is not as good a cure as they thought." She shook her head as she prepared to go down to dinner.

After Oma was gone, Meg pulled the large rocking chair over to the bay windows and sat in pure misery. What a wretched turn of events. Why did he have to come here? Why?

Meg never knew when she dozed off. The next thing she knew, Oma was coming in the door, talking as she came. "My little Margaret. Such a good time you missed at dinner. A boy, nice as any meatpacking boy I've ever met. He comes to our table and sits right at the side to me."

Seeing Meg's sleepy expression, she said, "I woke you. I am so sorry." She drew off her gloves and lay them with her fan on the marble-top bureau. "You have a nice rest?"

"I think so. Now what were you saying?"

"The boy at dinner." Oma pulled up a chair next to Meg. "He arrives just today."

Surely Oma couldn't be talking about. . .

"He knows a little German. So funny it was to hear him say the words. Best as he can, though. He tries. He has nice manners. Courteous to me, an old lady. And a sense of humor as well. A lonely orphan he is. Lives with his uncle."

"Tell me his name, Oma."

"Damon. Damon Pollard. But no mind." She reached over to pat Meg's hand. "You will meet him at breakfast. I tell him my granddaughter is here. Now you will have a friend here your age."

Meg sat stunned. She could hardly believe what she was hearing. Damon had talked with kindness to Oma Schiller, a German woman? None of the boys in her class at school would have done such a thing.

Oma had asked that the kitchen help send up a plate of fruit for Meg, of which she ate every bite before retiring. Her mind, however, wasn't on food, but on a million other things. How could she have been so wrong?

After Oma was settled into a deep sleep, Meg sat gazing out the window at the moonlit hills. How silly she'd been. And how selfish. She'd been so caught up in fear of what Damon might think of her, she hadn't even given him a chance. She'd not considered that the boy might be lonely. That he might need a friend.

Fear. A paralyzing thing. She'd been fearful of so many

things. Afraid to stand up to Fred's attacks. Afraid to admit to Mama that she was truly ill. Afraid to ask for permission to visit the art gallery. Afraid to stand up for what she believed. Afraid, even, to enter the art contest.

Why, she'd even been ashamed of her own grandparents because of fear of ridicule. How foolish she'd been.

Suddenly, Meg saw things so clearly. She remembered her fear of the old hens and how the mitt—her own idea—had helped her conquer that fear. God surely wanted her to conquer the other fears in her life as well. Susannah had constantly encouraged her to stand up for what she believed. With God's help, Meg was determined to do just that.

The next morning at breakfast, Meg wasn't surprised when a dark-haired, dark-eyed young man approached their table. Before Oma could introduce them, Damon said simply, "Hello, Meg. Good to see you again."

Oma's eyes grew wide. "You know my Margaret?"

"We've met briefly," he said, his eyes dancing. "May I sit down?"

"Please do," Oma said, waving to a chair.

Turning to Meg, he said. "I found this on the veranda when I first arrived yesterday." He reached into the pocket of his coat. "Somehow I think it might belong to you."

Damon unfolded a piece of paper on which, among other sketches, was a likeness of Damon.

Meg's face grew hot as she realized it must have dropped from her things in her hurry to go inside. But before she could speak, Oma said. "Margaret did this?" She took the paper from Damon's hands. "Why, drawing is good." She looked at Damon. "This looks much like you."

134

"I agree. Much like me." He smiled at Meg, putting her at ease and making her forget her embarrassment.

"I didn't know I dropped it. Thank you," she said taking it from Oma.

"I could show you a few techniques to improve if you'd like."

Meg brightened, then stopped. "Oh, I wouldn't want to put you to the bother."

"No bother at all. Uncle Jack sent me up here to rest, and I don't think I even need a rest."

"The young man's uncle runs some art institute," Oma said as the steward brought another dish full of cheese and fruit to their table.

"Yes, Oma," Meg said. "I know. Our class visited the institute, and I saw him there."

Oma nodded and went back to her breakfast. Meg hoped Damon would say nothing about the day of the blizzard. He didn't, but as they ate, Damon asked questions about their family. Oma added bits and pieces here and there, inserting the fact that none of the Allerton grandchildren could speak German and what a shame that was.

Once the rising sun had warmed the veranda, many of the guests chose to spend the morning hours out there or on the front lawns or strolling through the gardens.

Damon suggested they go to a table at the far corner of the veranda where they could spread out paper and work. Oma served as their very proper chaperone. The hours flew by as Damon showed Meg techniques with pen, with the pastels, and even a few tricks with the colored pencils. Meg was delirious with joy. And all the while they worked, Damon talked. He talked as though he'd not had someone to talk to for ever so long.

"Uncle Jack brought me to Cincinnati to mentor me in painting, but also to tutor me in my studies. Though I love Uncle Jack and he's very kind to me, I would much rather attend a public school."

Meg began to realize that Damon was a boy very much like Stephen. Why had she been so afraid of him? Fear, she could see, shut her off from so many things.

That evening as she and Oma were preparing to go to supper, Meg opened her heart and shared with Oma her deep love for art. Then, taking a deep breath, she told how she had slipped away to the institute in the snowstorm. That she'd gone specifically to see Damon's showing.

"Emma, she tells me the blizzard catch you. It was clear to me you didn't go right home. I trusted you to tell me in your own time."

"But there's more. Being in the storm made me sick, and being sick has put a hardship on everyone on the family. Even you. I feel terrible about all of it."

Oma came to Meg and patted her shoulder. "Little Meg. Like the bending willows. Some bending is good, my little fawn, some is bad. You bend too much!"

A willow? Meg wondered if that was like the bruised reed that Aunt Lucy talked about.

"Doctor tells your mama and your papa you have been sick for a long time. Not just from time in a blizzard."

"A long time?"

Oma nodded. "Tell me if it is not so."

Meg thought a moment. Was that why she was weak and headachy so much? "Yes, Oma. Perhaps it is so. But I never wanted to admit I felt bad. It seemed wrong."

"Is never wrong to be honest. Your mama hurts deep inside that she did not know."

"Mama hurts because I'm sick?" Meg could hardly believe it.

"She loves you very much, as do I."

Meg put her arms about Oma and hugged her tight. What a wonderful trip this was turning out to be.

Through the remainder of their stay, Meg had her own private art lessons each day. Her confidence in her work grew as Damon praised her efforts. Each day she and Damon came to know one another better. Oma had been right about his humor. His wit was lively and he loved a good joke. Meg found herself laughing more than she had in a very long time.

One afternoon as she was describing Fred to Damon, she mentioned his love of science and his admiration for inventors such as Samuel Morse.

Damon nodded. "Sam Morse, the artist? Yes, I know him."

"No, no. I'm speaking of the man who invented the telegraph. Fred admires him greatly."

"He's one and the same."

Meg laughed at the irony. "You mean the scientist is also an artist?"

"Morse was a personal friend of two of my uncles, and one uncle tutored him in portrait painting. I've met Mr. Morse on a number of occasions. Sam Morse has painted the portraits of Eli Whitney and Daniel Webster and many others. Does that seem strange to you?"

"Strange? Not to me. But it will help me greatly in dealing with my younger brother." She went on to explain about Fred and his relentless teasing, saying drawing was a waste of time. "Something like this could change many things back home."

"I'd be glad to tell Fred all about old Sam. Think that might help?"

Meg laughed. "I think it would help a great deal. It would take some of the wind out of Fred's sails."

By the time Meg and Oma were ready to leave Yellow Springs to return home, Meg could hardly believe she'd ever been afraid of Damon Pollard. Now she couldn't wait to get home and tell Susannah and Stephen all about her new friend.

Meg wanted to tell Susannah that she was ready to enter the art contest as well. And that she was ready to stand up for what she believed.

Chapter 17

A New Meg

Upon Meg's first day back at school, she went to Mr. Gallagher to ask for a form to enter the art contest. Susannah was thrilled.

"Something's happened to you, Meg," she said. "You look healthy again, but it's more than that."

Meg just smiled. "You've been trying to tell me to stand up for what I believe, Susannah. With God's help, I'm doing just that."

Dr. Logan was pleased with Meg's progress. His further orders to her were "In the future, when you feel bad, you must rest." To Mama he said, "Emma, you may be able to work relentlessly, but your daughter cannot. God created her a little differently."

Mama nodded and looked at Meg. "I know now, Dr. Logan."

Meg and Mama had already had a long talk, in which Mama had asked Meg to forgive her for not realizing she was truly sick. Then Meg asked Mama to forgive her for going to the institute without permission. They had hugged and wept together.

After being pronounced well, Meg asked Mama to have a dinner for the Hendrickses and Damon. To Meg's delight, Mama agreed.

Meg had been right about Fred. He was impressed beyond words that Damon personally knew an inventor. Damon helped him see that art was not all that far removed from science. Meg was sure Fred would never tease her again about her drawings.

And to her delight, Damon and Stephen became fast friends. Within a couple weeks of meeting the Hendrickses, Damon was spending afternoons helping out at the mercantile.

Spring returned to the city with a flourish. Flowering trees were transformed into pink and white explosions of color. The oaks and maples were budding, and flowers bloomed on every corner. Meg wanted to paint everything she saw.

One evening Meg mustered the courage to ask Papa if she could speak to him alone. Papa raised his craggy brows. "This sounds important. Shall we meet in the parlor?"

Once Papa had closed the door and they were settled in the overstuffed chairs, Papa said, "What is it, Meg? What did you want to talk about?"

Taking a breath and fighting down fear, Meg said, "Papa,

your craftsmanship in your furniture making is very important to you. But my art is important to me as well. Would you allow me to study art? To take lessons?"

Papa thought a moment. "Meg, people need beds and bureaus and secretaries. These are necessary items."

"But doesn't a work of art enhance a lovely piece of furniture? Think of how the two go together in the fine homes where your furniture is found. As you say, there may not be a *need* for art, but God created exquisite spring flowers. Can you think of a need for them?"

Papa said nothing for a time, but Meg could tell he was thinking.

In the silence, Meg thought of Fred and his dreams. She added, "And Fred's dream of a steam-driven lathe is as important to him as my art is to me. I know that hand-carved furniture is your trademark, but does it have to be one or the other? Couldn't it be both? Couldn't there be a part of the factory that is mechanized and a part where the hand carving is done? Wouldn't it be better for you to utilize Fred's wonderful talents than have him work for someone else?"

Meg could hardly believe she'd said that much and said it so clearly. Papa must have been surprised as well. "I've always known you had a good head on your shoulders, Margaret. Tell Fred to come in here, and let's all have a good long talk."

As Meg went to fetch her brother, she knew Aunt Lucy had been right. There was more than one way to be strong.

CHAPTER 18

The Prize

The large meeting hall at the institute was crowded with students, teachers, and parents. Meg sat beside Susannah in the third row. She smoothed the skirt of her silk dress and fought the butterflies in her stomach.

Susannah reached over and squeezed Meg's hand, then whispered, "I'm so proud of you."

"Your prayers have helped me so much," Meg whispered back.

President Foote was on the podium, calling the audience to order. He was ready to unveil the winning entries. Meg had learned a few days ago that her landscape of the hills around Yellow Springs had won first place in her division.

It was then that she learned the best news of all. Not only would her work hang in the gallery, but she would also receive free art lessons through the summer—lessons taught in part by Robert Scott Duncanson. After that news, Papa could hardly say no to her taking lessons, but Meg was still glad she'd spoken to him before she knew. Perhaps her days of being controlled by fear were behind her.

Nervously, she went over her acceptance speech in her mind. At last the moment came. As her landscape was unveiled, there were ooh's from the audience and warm applause. *"Yellow Springs*, by Margaret Allerton," announced President Foote.

That was Meg's cue to come to the podium. As she did, Damon, who sat on the podium right beside Mr. Duncanson, gave her a bright smile. She smiled back. Without his teaching, she might never have received this high honor.

At the lectern, she gazed out over the audience. Mrs. Gravitt looked as proud as if she'd done the painting herself. There were all the Hendrickses, each of whom had been such a support to her. Beside them were Oma and Opa, sitting as close as two lovebirds. Meg felt she knew them now as real people.

Mama had tears in her eyes, and Papa was patting her hand. Julia gave a small wave and big smile.

Then Meg looked at Fred. Her brother had been busy the past few weeks drawing plans for stationary steam engines. Never had she seen him so excited. He smiled up at her and gave her a big wink.

Spreading out her notes, Meg began her speech.

There's More!

The American Adventure continues with *Enemy or Friend.* Fred Allerton has a problem. His father refuses to trust him with the very machines Fred built to make their furniture factory work faster. Then Father hires a man to supervise Fred. It soon becomes clear to everyone but Father that Mr. Purlee doesn't know what he's doing. Even worse in Fred's eyes is the fact that Mr. Purlee helps slave owners.

Fred's problems follow him home, where his sister Julia is becoming close friends with Mr. Purlee's daughters and refuses to listen to Fred's warnings about them.

When Mr. Purlee blames an explosion in the factory on Fred and Father believes the man, Fred leaves home to live with his cousin Tim. Will Father and Fred settle their differences? And how can Fred's enemy possibly become a friend?